A Dream of Madness

James Pattinson

First published in 1987 by Robert Hale Limited.

This edition published in 2018 by Endeavour Media Ltd.

Table of Contents

Chapter One – NEW TENANT

It was called Raven House; nobody knew why. At least, none of its present inhabitants did; but they were all late-comers to the property and for them anything more than ten years ago was lost in the mists of antiquity. Not that they would have been interested anyway; they had more pressing matters to occupy their minds; chief of which was the ever-present problem of making one pound do the work of two.

There were certainly no ravens in the house now, with or without the capital letter. There was a bird named Rita Woolley, but she was of the human variety. She occupied a bed-sitting-room on the second floor and there were only the attics above that. Miss Woolley was twenty-two years old and had blonde hair and a good figure and managed somehow to keep up her spirits even in somewhat adverse circumstances.

She had been in and out of quite a number of jobs, mostly of the secretarial kind, and when, as now, she had nothing going in this line she contrived to keep her head above water with the help of the Department of Health and Social Security. She had hopes that things would pick up, but meanwhile she spent a fairly large proportion of her time in and about Raven House and was a keen observer of all that went on in that none too desirable residence.

The house was at the end of a row and had probably looked rather imposing before it had become so dilapidated. In this dilapidation it was not alone; it matched the rest of the houses in the row, and there was a general impression of decay and dinginess about them all, as though a kind of structural blight had descended on the street.

Clyde Fawley arrived one day in early spring and moved into a room on the same floor as Miss Woolley's; just across the landing in fact. It had become vacant when the previous occupant, a part-time barman, had decided to try his fortune in a different part of the world. Fawley was an American; twenty-four years old, black-haired and not at all bad-looking; as Miss Woolley observed when she first set eyes on him. He was also a well set-up young man, though perhaps a trifle lean, and there was a certain air of intensity about him which Miss Woolley did not fail to notice, for she was in her way something of a student of the male sex in general and handsome young members of it in particular.

When she spotted Clyde Fawley he was just coming up the stairs with Mr Drane, the agent who saw about letting the rooms and the collection of the rents. Mr Drane was a middle-aged bulbous person with a spotty face and a complexion rather like dough that had been kneaded with grubby hands. He always dressed in a shapeless grey suit of indeterminate age, black shoes, a greasy raincoat and a wide-brimmed hat of a type that had gone out of fashion before the start of World War Two. One word described him to a nicety: it was "seedy". Herbert Drane was seediness personified.

Miss Woolley waited on the landing for the two men to complete their ascent, as though a certain natural modesty restrained her from passing them on the stairs.

"Good morning, Mr Drane," she said; though she was not looking at him but at the younger man who was following at his heels.

Drane made a grunting sound which might have been taken to be an acknowledgement of the greeting. He was wheezing slightly after the climb and he stared glumly and perhaps a trifle disapprovingly at the young woman. He was not a popular visitor to Raven House because he usually came demanding money and threatening dire consequences if it was not immediately forthcoming. The fact that he was not himself the landlord but merely an employee of that invisible personage made no difference; his face was not welcome inside those walls.

Clyde Fawley glanced at Miss Woolley, but it was impossible to tell from his expression whether or not he was favourably impressed by what he saw. He was wearing blue jeans and a Harris tweed jacket with leather elbow patches and was carrying a large and rather travel-worn suitcase which apparently contained all his luggage.

Miss Woolley seized the opportunity of making herself known to him. "Hello there! Looks like you and me are going to be neighbours if you're moving into Smithy's old room. My name's Rita – Rita Woolley."

Mr Drane cut in testily: "Mr Fawley hasn't decided to take the room yet. He hasn't even seen it. He may not like it."

Miss Woolley smiled sweetly. "Oh, but I'm sure he will. It's such a nice room. They all are in this house, aren't they, Mr D?"

Drane ignored the sarcasm. Miss Woolley was needling him, but he did not react: years of rent-collecting had thickened his skin until it was impervious to all such verbal darts as this.

"Come along, Mr Fawley," he said. "This way, if you please."

He unlocked a door and went into a room with Clyde Fawley close behind.

"Well, there it is."

It was a fairly large room, with a window looking out on to a back garden in which a few neglected shrubs and a lot of coarse grass and weeds were making a vain attempt to hide the piles of junk that had been dumped there. The room was furnished after a fashion; the main items being a divan-bed, a wardrobe, a chest of drawers, a table and a pair of armchairs. In an alcove were a gas-cooker and a sink, some shelves and a rather dingy refrigerator.

Fawley gave a cursory glance all around. Then he nodded.

"It'll do."

"So you'll take it?"

"Sure."

"A wise decision. You won't find anything better. Not without paying through the nose. It's a low rental."

"So you told me."

Fawley took a wallet from his pocket, extracted some banknotes and handed them to Drane, who made an entry in a rent book and gave the book to the new tenant.

"I hope you'll be comfortable here, Mr Fawley. If there's any little problem just get in touch. I'll see what I can do."

Drane was edging towards the door, anxious to get away.

"I'll do that," Fawley said: but Drane was already out of the room and closing the door behind him.

It was about two minutes later when there was a light tap on the door and Rita Woolley stepped into the room without waiting for an invitation. Fawley was unpacking his suitcase and putting things in the wardrobe. He turned and looked at the girl but said nothing, waiting for her to speak. And she was not slow in doing so.

"Just thought I'd pop in and see how you were settling in. I saw old Drane going away alone, so I guessed you'd decided to take the room. I thought you would."

"Yes?" Fawley said.

"Oh, yes. I mean to say, it's not so bad really, is it?"

"Could be worse, I guess."

"You bet it could. You should see the places some people live in in this enlightened country. Not fit for pigs. You intending to stay here long?"

"I don't know. It depends on circumstances. Maybe so, maybe not."

She caught the accent. "You're American, aren't you?"

"Yes."

"That's great. I just love Americans. What's your first name, Mr Fawley?"

"It's Clyde, but –"

"Clyde! Oh, that's nice. It's got a sort of romantic sound to it, don't you think?"

"I don't know. I've never thought about it."

"You can call me Rita if you like."

"Well, thanks," Fawley said. But he was not sure he wanted to accept the invitation; he was wary of Miss Woolley's advances. He remembered what Duggan had said to him about relations with the Brits; that was his word for the British people, a pejorative term spoken with a kind of contemptuous disdain and an ugly twist of the lips. Duggan had given him a warning to be careful about whom he talked to; to avoid all intimate contacts; to keep himself to himself and a guard on his tongue. Fawley intended taking the advice because, though he was not at all sure he cared much for Pat Duggan, the man had certainly had experience and was a tough character who knew his way around. Fawley himself on the other hand, though not lacking in enthusiasm and dedication, was a greenhorn in this particular game; and he knew it.

Nevertheless, with the best intentions in the world, he found it difficult to repel Miss Woolley. He might have told her bluntly that he wanted nothing to do with her and that he would be obliged if she would get the hell out of it; but the fact was that he was by nature an easy-going friendly sort of person and it was not in his character to behave with such blatant rudeness towards anyone, and especially a young woman with such undoubted physical charm.

He saw that he ought to have locked the door after the departure of Mr Drane, but it simply had not occurred to him to do so. And who could have anticipated that she would have walked straight in like this?

"Have you got a job or something over here?" Miss Woolley inquired.

"No. Well, not exactly."

"Not exactly! That sounds mysterious?" She regarded him with an expression that had about it a certain archness. "You know, Clyde, I think there's more to you than meets the eye."

He answered quickly, as though eager to dispel any such thought: "No; you're wrong, quite wrong. There's no mystery about it. The truth is, I'm writing a book. I'm here to gather background material."

It was partly the truth; he was indeed working, though none too diligently, on a novel. He had a notebook in the suitcase and now and then he added a few more words to those he had already written. But it was just a hodgepodge of ideas with no real plot and he doubted whether anything worthwhile would ever come of it.

For as long as he could remember he had had this dream of being a writer; it had fascinated him, though he could not have said why. And the hard fact was that he had never had a single piece of writing published; he had hammered out poems and essays and short stories, yet not one of them had ever appeared in all the glory of the printed word. But still the dream would not go away. It existed side by side with that other, sterner dream that possessed his mind; and perhaps one day the two would mingle to produce a work of truly epic proportions; a thing of blood and beauty that might astonish the world. Some day!

He became aware that Rita Woolley was speaking again. "A writer! Oh, my! Think of that in Raven House!" She seemed to be greatly impressed, and Fawley had a slight feeling of guilt because his words had obviously led her to believe that he was an established author. "We've never had anybody like that here before. You must be very clever."

"Oh, I wouldn't say that."

"Now you're being modest. I don't do a lot of reading myself; just the women's magazines and suchlike when there's nothing better to do. Can't remember when I last read a real book. I suppose I'm just a pin-brain really." She tapped her forehead. "Nothing much up here, you know."

"I'm sure that's not so," Fawley said. But he guessed she might be telling the truth at that. "Maybe you don't have a lot of spare time for reading."

Miss Woolley gave a wry smile. "I wish I could honestly say that was the reason, but I can't. The fact is I'm one of the three million plus."

Fawley looked puzzled. "Three million?"

"The unemployed. I'm currently out of a job, so I've got all the spare time that's going."

"Oh, I'm sorry. I didn't know."

"No way you could. Don't let it bother you. It doesn't bother me. I look upon it as a purely temporary inconvenience."

Fawley closed the wardrobe door and wondered how to get rid of his visitor. But he was saved the embarrassment of asking her to leave.

"Well," she said, "I mustn't hang around here all day. I expect you have lots to do."

"Yes," Fawley said. "I do have a few things to see to."

Miss Woolley moved towards the door. "I won't stop you then. Just thought it would be a good idea for us to get acquainted, seeing as we're going to be living so close."

"Glad you did." It was not quite the truth. Fawley was being polite.

"If there's anything I can do to help you feel at home, just say the word. You know where I live."

"Well, thanks, but –"

"Anything," Miss Woolley said, "anything." She hovered in the doorway a few moments, as if waiting for Fawley to say something; but he just looked at her in silence and finally she backed out of the room and closed the door.

Fawley breathed a sigh of relief, crossed to the door and turned the key in the lock to ensure that nobody else could walk in without waiting for an invitation.

Having thus made sure of his privacy he finished unpacking the suitcase. When he had removed all the clothing and various other items there remained only one other thing in the case, a small green plastic bag fastened with a zipper. He picked up the bag, which was rather heavy for its size, and placed it on the table. Then he slid back the zipper and took from the bag a black self-loading pistol. It was a deadly-looking weapon, a nine-millimetre Browning; no toy but a real man-killer.

Fawley handled the pistol like a man who was familiar with such weapons, and if Miss Woolley had walked in and seen him now she might have been forced to make a swift revision of that initial impression she had gained with regard to this new tenant of the bed-sitting-room that had formerly been occupied by the part-time barman named Smith. She might even have decided that Clyde Fawley was a man it would be advisable to leave very much to his own devices; because people who carried nine-millimetre pistols around in their luggage were unlikely to be doing so just for the fun of it.

Miss Woolley might or might not have been, as she herself said, a pin-brain, but she probably had enough sense to realize that such people could cause a load of trouble, not only for themselves but also for those with whom they came in contact. And if there was one thing she could very well do without, it was trouble. Trouble might come to you whether you wanted it or not, but only a complete idiot would go round looking for it.

But Miss Woolley was not going to walk into the room for the very good reason that the door was locked. She was not going to see the gun in Fawley's hand or the intense, almost crazed look in his eyes, the hardened jaw and tightened lips, which made him seem an altogether different person from the soft-spoken, apparently mild young man to whom she had introduced herself.

The change was only momentary. It was as if the feel of the pistol had triggered something in his brain; a thought, a vision perhaps, which came and was gone. Then his grip on the weapon relaxed and he put it back in the plastic bag.

Chapter Two – LESSONS

Clyde Fawley had certainly had plenty of experience in the handling of pistols; and he was no novice with a rifle either. For this fact one man could undoubtedly claim the credit, or, as some people might have said, the blame. This man was Fawley's uncle, Daniel O'Higgins.

Uncle Danny was an elder brother of Clyde's mother, an Irish-American remarkable chiefly for just two things: the business acumen that had helped him to amass a considerable fortune in US dollars and the abiding hatred which he entertained for the British people and all their works.

Daniel Reilly O'Higgins was one of those Americans who, though having been born in New York and lived there all their lives, yet seemed to be still dwelling spiritually in the Ireland of their ancestors. To him the depredations of Cromwell's brutal soldiery, the suffering of the years of famine when the potatoes rotted in the ground and relief was denied to the starving people by the British Government, the atrocities committed by the Black and Tans and all the other ills visited upon a persecuted nation by that other, more powerful nation across the Irish Sea were not matters of ancient history long since past and done with but events that had occurred only yesterday. Indeed, they were still happening, for was it not a fact there was even now a British army of occupation in Northern Ireland, which was there for the one purpose only of maintaining the supremacy of the Protestant interlopers over the struggling Catholic natives?

Clyde's father, Henry Fawley, who could claim no Irish ancestry and was a rather staid insurance broker, made no secret of the fact that in his opinion Daniel O'Higgins was as crazy as a coot.

"How a reasonably intelligent woman like you, Maggie," he once said to his wife, "ever came to have a brother like that hare-brained idiot beats me, it really does. The man's a lunatic, a raving lunatic; you know he is."

Margaret Fawley was in the habit of making some mild protest at such extreme remarks. "Now, now, Henry," she would say, "you shouldn't be too hard on him. Danny was always a wild sort of boy, but his heart is in the right place."

She was ten years younger than her brother and as a child had worshipped him; but she did not share his strong views on the Irish question and was not a little concerned to observe how much influence he had over her son. Clyde was so impressionable and Danny had a persuasive way with him.

"Where's the good of having a heart in the right place if your brains are addled?" Henry Fawley wanted to know. "He ought to see a shrink. He should be shut up in a padded cell. He isn't fit to be walking around with normal people."

All of which was something of an exaggeration, since Daniel O'Higgins was manifestly as sharp-witted as they came and had the Midas touch in the world of property dealing, where you had to be pretty smart to stay ahead of the field. He was a big bluff man, self-confident and extrovert; all that Henry Fawley, with his rimless glasses, his smooth pale cheeks and immaculate fingernails, so obviously was not.

Clyde Fawley was captivated by Uncle Danny at an early age and grew up completely under the influence of this man who seemed to him to be cast in the mould of all the heroes of song and legend. In comparison his father appeared colourless and insipid, even despicable. Clyde wished he could have been Uncle Danny's son; but O'Higgins was not married. A wife, he said, would have cramped his style; he needed to be free from all domestic ties.

As it was Clyde enjoyed almost all the advantages he would have had if he had indeed been O'Higgins's son. Uncle Danny was generous with money and other gifts, and Clyde had the freedom of his large New York house, where there were servants to wait upon him and treat him like a young lord.

As he grew older Clyde spent so much time at his uncle's place and in the property dealer's company that Henry Fawley began to raise objections. He spoke about it to his wife.

"The boy's seeing far too much of that brother of yours. I don't like it. It's bad for him, the influence of that man."

Though Margaret Fawley did to some extent share her husband's concern she did her best to soothe him. "Oh, I'm sure there's no harm in it. And after all it's only natural that Danny should take an interest in his nephew; he's got no one else. It could turn out to Clyde's advantage in the end."

"That's a pretty mercenary way of looking at it. What you're saying is that Clyde could come into the O'Higgins dollars. Is that it?"

"I wouldn't put it quite like that."

"How would you put it?"

She sidestepped the question. "Well, we have to be practical, don't we? And anyway, what can we do about it? Surely you aren't proposing to forbid Clyde to visit his own uncle."

"It mightn't be such a bad idea at that," Fawley said. But he knew it was not on. He was no heavy-handed Victorian parent and on this issue he could not have counted on the unquestioning support of his wife.

He thought of having a heart-to-heart talk with his son; and he might have done so if he had believed it would have been of any use. But the plain fact was that he and Clyde had never had a very happy relationship; there seemed to be an invisible barrier between them which had grown more and more insurmountable with the passing of time. Anything he might have said, any warning he might have given regarding Daniel O'Higgins would, he was certain, have been received in a stony silence which would enrage and baffle him. These days he just could not get through to the boy.

"It's my opinion that Daniel is getting far too strong a hold on him. He's at an impressionable age."

"But no harm will come of it, I'm sure. Clyde's a sensible boy, and when he goes up to college things will be different."

Fawley hoped so. The wider interests of the campus life might act as a counterweight to the O'Higgins influence. Maturity would surely open the boy's eyes to the craziness of his uncle's views, and he would then have enough sense to recognize that the man had a bee in his bonnet.

What neither Henry nor Margaret Fawley realized was just how strong a grip O'Higgins had taken on his nephew's mind. They could not guess, for Clyde had never confided in them, how thoroughly O'Higgins had infected the youngster with his own obsession: this dream of an Ireland from which the alien oppressor had been finally cast out. And to O'Higgins's way of thinking there was only one means by which this object could possibly be achieved: force of arms; arms in the hands of the Provisional IRA.

"They're the boys who are doing the fighting, Clyde. They're in the front line and I honour them for it. They need our help; they deserve our help; and by God, if Daniel O'Higgins has any say in the matter they'll get our help. They'll get it come hell or high water."

It enraged him to observe the supine attitude of the US Government to the IRA, the way it sided with the British in trying to defeat those brave lads who were simply fighting for the right to be free. Even the FBI had been brought in to prevent shipments of arms getting through to the Provisionals. And yet there had been a time when the Americans themselves had been in the same situation as the Catholics in Ulster; they themselves had once been oppressed by the English and had had to fight for their independence. There were people in Washington who seemed to have forgotten the history of their own country, goddamn it!

Clyde Fawley, perhaps because of the awareness that the pure Irish blood in his veins had been contaminated by the intermingling of the alien Fawley variety, was for this very reason eager to prove that he was nevertheless a true son of Erin. He accepted the O'Higgins doctrine without question and longed to strike a blow for those heroic brethren on the far side of the Atlantic in that small green island from which so much that was best in the American nation had originally sprung. One day – and it could not be too soon – perhaps he would.

Daniel O'Higgins had introduced his nephew to the world of firearms at a fairly tender age. In the basement of the grand residence on Riverside Drive there was a small arsenal of handguns and sporting rifles, as well as a target range where the weapons could be fired. As soon as he reckoned Clyde was big enough to handle a gun O'Higgins took him down to the basement and gave him his first lesson, using one of the smaller calibre pistols which would not break his wrist as a Colt forty-five might have done. There would be time to work up to the really lethal pieces in the armoury as the boy grew up.

To his great satisfaction Clyde took to guns as small girls take to dolls and older girls to ponies; he was fascinated by them. To him the basement of the mansion on Riverside Drive was a treasure-house of rare delights. There was nothing remotely like it in the more modest dwelling across the Hudson River in Brooklyn where he had been brought up; and it was hardly to be expected that there would have been, for such things were not in Henry Fawley's line.

Uncle Danny did not expressly warn Clyde not to tell his parents about the guns and the firing-range, but he gave a pretty strong hint that it might be advisable to keep the information to himself. The hint was scarcely necessary; Clyde had long since given up confiding in his father on any subject and he had enough sense to realize that his mother would hardly be overjoyed to learn that her son was being trained in the use of deadly weapons. She was a peace-loving woman and shared none of those wild dreams regarding the land of her ancestors which so obsessed her brother.

O'Higgins congratulated his nephew on the way in which he was picking up the skills of pistol-shooting. "You're a natural born gunslinger, Clyde my boy. You have the hand and you have the eye. You'll be a credit to your old Uncle Danny, that's for sure."

"I'll try to be," Clyde said. And he meant it.

When he grew older O'Higgins took him on hunting trips. O'Higgins owned a lakeside cabin in the Adirondack Mountains. He had a canoe and he and Clyde paddled their way along the river that flowed into the lake. They shot at almost anything that moved and camped out under the stars. Clyde loved it all.

But he told his parents nothing of this either. They were under the impression that the purpose of the visits to the cabin in the Adirondacks was fishing, a harmless enough pastime in Henry Fawley's estimation, even though he could see no attraction in it himself. Stalking game with a hunting rifle was something very different, and neither he nor his wife would have been at all happy about that.

O'Higgins was full of praise for the boy. Under his tuition Clyde was coming along just as he would have wished; he saw his nephew as an extension of his own ego, a means of self-fulfilment. He had a dream and Clyde was the chosen instrument to make that dream a reality. He might himself have taken the necessary action if it had not been for the handicap of age. This at least was the reason he formed in his own mind, refusing to face the uncomfortable fact that even if he had been younger he might not have had the courage to leave the safety of the United States and plunge into the perils that would be lying in wait on the other side of the ocean.

It was apparent to him that Clyde had no such qualms; the boy's enthusiasm had been aroused by the glib tongue of his mentor and he could hardly wait for the day when he would be in a position to strike a blow in the cause of Ireland's freedom. Already he shared O'Higgins's dream and had no suspicion that he might be following a chimera; that indeed it might be nothing but a dream of madness formed in the eccentric brain of an ageing fanatic. To Clyde Fawley, Daniel O'Higgins was the only true prophet and he the devoted disciple.

College made no difference to the relationship. On the campus Clyde made no close friends; he was regarded as something of a loner, even a bit of a screwball in fact. People found him pleasant in manner and physically attractive, but always there seemed to be an invisible barrier which he had erected around himself, as though he was wary of forming any intimate relationship with his fellow students, either male or female. They thought it strange perhaps, but how were they to know that he had devoted himself to a cause, had dedicated his life to it; and that the cause was paramount?

He left college with an arts degree but with no intention of following an academic career. And he had no need to search for employment, since there was an appointment waiting for him in the O'Higgins business whenever he should choose to take it up. Henry Fawley did not approve and Mrs Fawley had misgivings; but Clyde was of age and free to make his own decisions; the most they could do was to try to dissuade him from taking such a step.

"With your qualifications," Fawley said, "surely you could do something better with your life."

"It's what I want to do," Clyde told him. "And how can you tell that anything else would be better?"

Fawley answered, with a burst of anger that was rare with him: "Nothing could be worse than working for that crack-brained old bastard, if you ask me."

Clyde was icy. "I am not asking you. You're prejudiced. You've never understood Uncle Danny; never wanted to."

"And you do understand him, I suppose?" Fawley inquired with a sneer.

"Yes, I do. And I can tell you he's a fine man. America could do with a few more like him."

"Well, God help America, that's all I can say. And if you're really so crazy about Mr Daniel O'Higgins maybe you'd better go and live with him."

"That's exactly what I intend to do," Clyde said. "He's offered to let me have a self-contained apartment in a wing of the house. It'll be just fine; I shall be able to come and go as I please."

"But Clyde, dear," Mrs Fawley protested. "You come and go as you please here. No one has ever stood in your way."

"It isn't the same thing."

"No, of course not." Fawley was sneering again. "This house isn't good enough for you, is it? You want something on a grander scale. The Riverside Drive style."

"That has nothing to do with it."

"I wish you'd think about it a little more," Mrs Fawley said. "It's not the sort of decision to take on the spur of the moment."

"I have thought about it. I'm convinced it will be best for all of us if I leave this house."

"But, Clyde –"

"Oh, let him go," Henry Fawley broke in testily. "Don't plead with him. It's perfectly obvious that his own parents mean less to him than that man's money."

"It's not the money I'm interested in," Clyde said.

"No? Then you're even more of a fool than I took you for."

With this parting shot Henry Fawley turned his back on his son and stalked out of the room. Clyde watched his departure with no feeling of regret. When the door had closed he turned to his mother.

"I'm sorry. Believe me, I don't want to hurt you; but this is the way it has to be."

She looked at him sadly. "What did we do wrong, Clyde? Tell me."

He did not answer the question; it would have been impossible to explain.

Chapter Three – ONE OF THE FACTS

Clyde Fawley's position in Daniel O'Higgins's business was a sinecure. He travelled around with his uncle, looked at property, met people, got to know how deals were made and so on; but he did no real work. It bothered him a little; he felt a slight pricking of the conscience because he was drawing a generous salary and was giving little in return. But when he mentioned it to O'Higgins his misgivings were dismissed with an airy wave of the hand.

"Don't let it worry you, Clyde my boy. I have plans for you. What's business? Just a way of lining your pocket; a means to an end. It's what we do with the money we make that counts."

Which was all very fine of course, but Clyde still felt that he ought to be doing rather more to earn his pay. Still, if Uncle Danny was happy why should he worry?

In the privacy of his apartment he did some writing, short pieces of prose and verse. He made a tentative start on a novel. He was still keeping his hand in with the guns in the basement and there was the occasional hunting expedition from the cabin by the lake in the Adirondacks. It was an easy life but he felt that it was simply the preparation for something else, something of far greater significance, something dangerous and possibly bloody, but nevertheless sublime.

O'Higgins introduced him to men who came to the house; Americans with Irish names. Some of them were hearty back-slapping men, but there were others who were quieter in their behaviour, men who spoke sparingly and seemed to pick their words with care, their eyes keen and probing. Clyde shook hands with them all and could sense that they were sizing him up, running a mental rule over him before deciding whether or not he was one of them, a person who could safely be trusted with compromising secrets.

Not that anything of this nature was ever discussed in his presence; it was as though he were serving a probationary period before being admitted as a full member into some kind of exclusive association. He accepted this apprenticeship, as it were, and looked forward to the day when he would be regarded by these men as an equal and a brother.

O'Higgins gave him encouragement. "They like you, Clyde. I've told them how good you are with guns. They think you're the right kind of material."

Clyde felt pleased. He did not ask what was meant by the right kind of material. He just knew that he had a mission and that the time would come when he would be told what he had to do. Meanwhile his duty was to keep himself in readiness.

There were women who occasionally came to the house on Riverside Drive; but not with the men. There was, O'Higgins said, a time for all things, and a bit of female company was good for a man now and then; it helped him to relax. The secret was never to become romantically involved; that was fatal.

Unfortunately, Clyde was at a more impressionable age than his uncle and he did become involved.

Her name was Jackie Dring and she was not much older than Clyde. She was small and dainty, with black hair cut in an urchin style, and there was a kind of elfin quality about her. Clyde Fawley was captivated by her, and suddenly the guns and the mission were forced into the background; now the only thing he wanted in life was this enchanting girl, and all else was of secondary importance.

Daniel O'Higgins was not slow to spot the way things were moving, and he was far from pleased. For the first time he saw his position threatened. A rival in the shape of an empty-headed slip of a girl was competing for the boy's allegiance, and if something were not quickly done to alter the situation all his treasured plans might be brought to nothing; the dream might never become reality.

But he was far too crafty to come out with any open opposition to his nephew's involvement with Miss Dring, for he knew that this might well prove counter-productive. He might have pointed out to Clyde that it was folly to go overboard for a common hooker; that the girl was only out for what she could get and had no more genuine feeling for him than for any other man she went to bed with; that nothing but disaster could stem from such a liaison and so on.

This was the kind of reasoned argument that should have been enough to convince any intelligent youngster that he was acting like a besotted idiot and ought to snap out of it pretty damn quick. Unfortunately, however, in such a situation intelligence was apt to count for nothing, and argument from older and wiser people tended only to make the person concerned all the more determined to go ahead and say to hell with the consequences. For when had any young man who fancied himself to he head over heels in love ever listened to the cold stern voice of reason?

So O'Higgins uttered not a single word of opposition when Clyde confided to him that he adored Miss Jackie Dring and hoped with as little delay as possible to marry her and presumably live happily ever after. Instead he was at pains to give the impression that he saw no reason at all why any young man should not get himself hitched up to a hooker if the hooker was willing.

Clyde winced at the word used to describe Miss Dring; it seemed to give him no little pain. "She'll be finishing with all that, of course. She was forced into it. She's had a hard life. You wouldn't believe."

O'Higgins reflected that the boy had never spoken a truer word; he would believe very little indeed that Miss Dring might say.

But all he said was: "I guess she has at that."

Clyde looked at him questioningly. "You're not mad at me, are you?"

"Now why would I be mad at you?" O'Higgins said.

"Well, it'll alter things, won't it? I mean, when I'm married I'll have responsibilities to my wife and possibly a family; so those plans we've made will have to be cancelled. It wouldn't be fair to her to do otherwise. You do see, don't you?"

"Sure, I see."

"And you don't mind?"

O'Higgins shrugged. "Well now, I'm not going to pretend it's not a disappointment; of course it is. But it's all a question of priorities and the way I look at it is this: the first priority is your welfare. If this is what you want; if this is what it takes to make you happy; okay." He gave Clyde a friendly pat on the shoulder. "It's your life, my boy, and you're the one that's got to make the choice."

Clyde was relieved; he had feared a stand-up fight, anger, recriminations. He would not have given way, of course, but he would have regretted having to fall out with his uncle. But it had not come to that; O'Higgins had been generous and understanding, and he loved him all the more for the way in which he had reacted to something that must have been a bitter disappointment to him.

"Thanks, Uncle Danny," he said. "You really are a great guy."

It was perhaps as well that he could not look into the great guy's mind and see what schemes were hatching there. It might have disillusioned him.

When he told Jackie that his uncle had raised no objection to the marriage she found it hard to believe. She had had more experience of life than Clyde Fawley and things had never come to her as easily as that; they had had to be fought for; nothing had ever been handed to her on a plate. So she was suspicious, looking for the catch.

Clyde was puzzled by her reaction; he had expected her to be delighted, but she seemed to be taking the news with very little evidence of joy.

"What's wrong?" he said. "I thought you'd be over the moon, but you don't look happy. This is what you want, isn't it?"

She kissed him. "Of course it is, but –"

"But what?"

"Oh, I don't know. It's just that I have this lousy feeling that something could still go wrong."

"Nothing will go wrong. You worry too much. And even if he hadn't given his blessing I'd still have married you. He doesn't own me, you know."

"But it wouldn't do to fall out with him, would it? How would you live?"

"I could get a different job."

"Could you?"

"Sure, I could. But why worry? I'm not going to need to. Everything's fine and dandy."

"Well, if you say so," she said. But she still sounded doubtful.

He could see that he had not succeeded in completely convincing her that all would go smoothly, but it made no difference; events would prove to her that he was right.

For him everything remained fine and dandy for just twenty-four hours; then it all came apart in his hands. At first he had no suspicion that anything was seriously wrong; he and Jackie had arranged to meet in the lobby of a Broadway theatre; a revival of "Oklahoma" was being staged and he had tickets for the show. He was not greatly surprised when she was not there at the appointed time; she was not the most punctual of persons and he did not begin to be uneasy until ten minutes had passed and she still had not put in an appearance.

The time for the curtain to go up arrived but no Miss Dring, and he was starting to worry. Suppose something had happened to her on the way to the theatre; an accident, a mugging, anything. He hung around for another half-hour, growing more and more jittery by the minute, before coming to the conclusion that it was useless to wait any longer, since it was obvious that she was not going to turn up.

He found a public telephone and rang through to her apartment, but there was no answer. Had she left the apartment or was she simply not taking any phone calls? Had something happened to make it impossible for her to do so? Suppose she had had a fall, broken a leg – suppose she was lying there unconscious – suppose –

He was really worried now, imagining all kinds of disasters that could have occurred. He hailed a cab and told the driver to take him to the address of the apartment, which was in a shabby old building in one of the less fashionable districts of Manhattan. It was on the second floor and he went up and rang the bell; but nobody opened the door. He rang again, with the same result. He tried the door, but it was locked. He felt an urge to put his shoulder to it and try to break it open, but he hesitated to take such drastic action, and as he was hesitating a woman came out of the adjoining apartment and spoke to him.

"If you're looking for Jackie," she said, "you're wasting your time. She left."

Fawley stared at her. "Left!" She was a blonde, thirtyish, full-blown and beginning to curl at the edges. "You mean she went out?"

"I mean left. She won't be coming back, I guess. She went with this man, see? Took her luggage and everything, like it was really final."

Fawley could not believe it. "Left with a man?"

"That's right. About forty, I'd say. Black hair, thinning on top. Moustache, dark complexion, with that kinda tough look. Bunchy shoulders, like there was a lot of muscle under the coat."

She had obviously taken careful note of the man, but it was not much help. "You don't know where they were going?"

"Sorry, no. They didn't confide in me."

Clyde Fawley was shattered. He simply did not understand. Why would she go away with a man when she should have been meeting him at the theatre? As far as he could see it made no sense at all.

*

It would have been less of a puzzle to Fawley if he had been present when the man called on Miss Dring earlier in the day. The man's name was Brogan and he was very persuasive. He offered money – quite a considerable sum – in exchange for Miss Dring's co-operation. It was such a lot of money that she would have found it difficult to refuse even if he had not hinted that a refusal might result in serious damage to her health, producing a gun from somewhere on his person to lend emphasis to the words and leave no doubt in the mind of the listener regarding their precise meaning.

Under the combined argument of the carrot and the stick she was unable to resist. Brogan did not say who he was working for, but there was no need for him to do so; she saw that she had been right to have doubts concerning Daniel O'Higgins's approval of the proposed marriage; he had just been uttering the words while all the time he had been turning over in his mind all possible ways of killing it off.

"I knew it," she said. "I just knew it would never work out."

But though she had known it she still felt regret. She and Clyde could have made a go of it if they had been allowed to, she was sure of it; he loved her and she was quite fond of him in her way. It would have worked. But not now.

"And don't ever try to get in touch with him," Brogan said. "You don't wanna go looking for trouble, do you?"

"No," Miss Dring said, "I don't."

There was no need. Trouble came looking for you. It was one of the facts of life.

*

When Clyde Fawley told his uncle that Jackie Dring had gone off with another man without so much as a word of farewell O'Higgins expressed surprise and sympathy. Fawley had no suspicion that it had all been arranged by O'Higgins himself; such an idea would never have entered his head.

O'Higgins could see how deeply the young man had been hurt by Miss Dring's conduct. He spoke bitterly of what he regarded as an inexplicable and unforgivable betrayal.

"I loved her. I thought she loved me. How could she do such a thing to me?"

"Women," O'Higgins remarked sententiously, "are strange creatures. A wise man doesn't put his trust in them."

"I believed in her. I would have trusted her with my life. And now this."

O'Higgins offered words of consolation. "I know, son. I know it hurts. I was young myself once, trusting, inexperienced. I got taken for a ride too. I know what it feels like. You think it's the end of the world, but it's not;

you get over it. And maybe it's all to the good, because you learn the lesson and you're wiser afterwards."

Fawley was not consoled. He doubted whether his uncle could ever have had the kind of feeling for a woman that he had had for Jackie; it was simply not conceivable. But in one respect at least O'Higgins was right: it was not the end of the world and he did get over it.

As a kind of reaction he went back with renewed enthusiasm to the guns and the dream, the things from which his love for Miss Dring had temporarily diverted him. And now there seemed to be an added determination, an increased fervour. It was as if he had purged himself of some weakness and was the stronger for it.

All of which Daniel O'Higgins observed with satisfaction, congratulating himself on the astute manner in which he had handled the crisis and brought about a happy outcome. He had no regrets; he had saved the boy from making a terrible mistake and had put him back on the right track.

He would get no thanks for what he had done, of course, but he wanted none; the knowledge that he had acted in the best interests of all concerned was sufficient reward. Now they could both get back to the important things in life.

Chapter Four – UNSATISFACTORY

The day Clyde Fawley met Michael Grady for the first time was like a landmark in the young man's life. Grady was in the library of the house on Riverside Drive when O'Higgins called Fawley in. There was no one else there; just this stranger sitting in one of the leather-upholstered armchairs with a glass of Irish whiskey on a small table by his elbow.

The library was a large room into which O'Higgins would take people on whom he wished to make an impression. It had oak-panelled walls and long rows of shelves filled with expensively-bound volumes which he never read. The particular visitor who was there now appeared completely unimpressed, however. In fact he seemed to regard the luxurious surroundings in which he found himself with a certain disdain, as though he despised this evidence of soft living which contrasted so sharply with the hard lot of the people he represented.

"Clyde," O'Higgins said, "I want you to meet Mr Michael Grady. Mr Grady, this is my nephew, Clyde Fawley, who I've told you about."

Fawley shook hands with the visitor. He knew who Grady was and why he was there; he was a representative of the Provisional IRA who had been sent to the United States to make arrangements for a shipment of arms and other supplies urgently needed for use in the fight against the British in Northern Ireland.

"I'm very pleased to meet you," Grady said. "Yer uncle tells me yer heart is in the good cause. Is that a fact?"

"It is," Fawley said.

He looked at Grady with a respect almost amounting to awe, as he might have regarded the hero of some old romance suddenly come to life before his eyes. He felt himself privileged to shake the hand of such a person, a hand that had perhaps fired a gun in support of that good cause of which the man had spoken.

Not that Grady looked much like a hero; at least not the romantic notion of one. He was a skinny little man with untidy black hair and a bald patch on the crown of his head. He had jug-handle ears and a snub nose and he wore a pair of glasses that had been mended with a piece of Scotch tape.

26

His suit was crumpled and it looked as if it had been slept in, as maybe it had. He was smoking a cigarette and dropping ash all down his shirt.

But when he spoke it was with an Irish brogue that was the genuine article and not like something put on by an American actor in a play by Sean O'Casey or J.M. Synge. Fawley was captivated by it.

"Well now, how fine it is to be meeting a young feller like you that's on our side, to be sure. Mr O'Higgins has put your feet on the right path, so he has."

"I've been a friend and guide," O'Higgins said with all due modesty. "But he took to it like a duck to water. Now he wants to be where the action is. Over there." He gave an airy wave of the hand to indicate the general direction of that part of the world he was referring to. "I guess you could use a volunteer?"

Grady did not exactly leap at the offer. "I'll be honest with you," he said. "It's not so much the front line troops as we're short of. There's a load of youngsters eager and willing to get in on the act. But it takes more than that; you need to have the aptitude."

"Clyde is apt. I give you my word on that."

Grady looked at Fawley. "I hope you've not got the notion that it's all fun and games like a cowboy movie. There's precious little fun and it's no bloody game. There's the soldier boys and the constabulary bastards chasing you on both sides of the border, and as like as not they'll blow your brains out first and ask questions afterwards."

"I didn't think it was a game," Fawley said. "I'm not afraid to take the risk."

"Are you not, then? Well, maybe so. But then again maybe you could change your mind when it's the reality of it that's staring you in the face. Meaning no disrespect to you, mind; but it's the background that counts. You've not been brought up to it like the lads from the Bogside and the Falls Road. You've not lived the rough life like they have."

"I've been on hunting trips in the Adirondacks," Fawley said. But he knew it was not the same thing, not by a mile. When Grady mentioned the Bogside and the Falls Road his pulse quickened, but he felt like an outsider. He had the impression that though Grady did not say it in so many words he was in fact mildly contemptuous of the offer that had been made. He was willing enough to take any amount of aid in the form of cash or arms or other supplies, but he was not really looking for any American

27

volunteers to fight on the streets of Derry or Belfast or in the border country between Ulster and the Republic.

"Hunting trips," Grady said, "is sport. There's a world of difference between killing animals and killing men."

"We know that," O'Higgins said. He was frowning slightly and Fawley could tell that he was none too pleased with the arguments Grady was putting forward. He was used to getting his own way and tended to resent any opposition. "But let's leave it for now. We'll talk about it later. Now if you're ready we'll go and take a look at the stuff."

"I'm ready," Grady said. He drank the remains of the whiskey and got up from his chair. "Lead the way."

*

O'Higgins drove, Grady sitting beside him and Fawley by himself on the back seat. The destination was probably unknown to Grady and it was certainly unknown to Fawley; never before had O'Higgins involved him quite so directly in the business that he was in the habit of referring to as Bundles for Britain. Fawley was not old enough to remember when the original Bundles for Britain scheme had been in operation in World War Two; it had been long before he had been born. And that scheme had been a more benevolent operation than the one O'Higgins now had in mind. His bundles were likely to be more lethal.

Fawley regarded being taken along with the two men as an indication that he was at last fully accepted as a member of the fraternity. He had guessed long ago that the group of Irish-American businessmen of which O'Higgins was one of the principal members organized a supply line to the Provisionals, but he had never been invited to take any part in the business himself. Perhaps O'Higgins had had to convince the other members of the association that his nephew was worthy of their trust, but now apparently he had succeeded in doing so.

It was an old warehouse down by the waterfront which they eventually came to, and there was a sign on the wall which read: Egerton Supply Company. There was a concrete enclosure in front with a couple of trailer units shunted away in one corner. Three cars were parked nearby and O'Higgins brought his Cadillac to a halt beside them. The warehouse doors were shut and there was no indication of any activity about the place; it looked dead.

"Let's go," O'Higgins said.

28

They all got out of the car and he led the way across the concrete. There was a wicket in one of the bigger doors and O'Higgins rapped on it with his knuckles. Someone on the other side asked who was there.

"It's Danny," O'Higgins said. "Open up."

The wicket was opened and they stepped inside, the man who had opened it closing and locking it behind them. Fawley recognized him as one of the visitors to his uncle's house who had been introduced as Mr Murphy. He was a dapper little man with a small moustache. He looked nervous.

There were three others and Fawley recognized them all, though the light inside the warehouse was none too good. Their names were McNulty, Cooney and Mitchell. O'Higgins introduced the man from Ireland and they all shook hands with him.

Mitchell laid a big blunt hand on Fawley's shoulder. "Welcome to the club, son. Nice to have you with us."

Fawley experienced a feeling of pride at being accepted by these men as an equal. But of course he wanted more than that. For men like these – solid, middle-aged American citizens – it might be enough to provide the Irish freedom fighters with the tools to do the job, but for a young man like him it was not enough by a long chalk; he needed to be nearer the action.

He heard Grady saying: "So let's be seeing what you have for us." And then they all began to move away from the door, walking down between the stacks of wooden crates that rose on each side like high walls.

The crates they finally came to were marked with the information that they contained spare parts for farm machinery and they were apparently destined for the Azores. Mitchell was carrying a case-opener and a claw-hammer and he levered the lid off one of the crates. Packed inside under a covering of thick felt were a number of Armalite rifles. Cooney lifted one of them out and handed it to Grady.

"You can use a few more of these, I guess?"

Grady handled the gun like a man who knew what he was doing. "We can always use jokers like this." He passed the rifle back to Cooney, who replaced it in the crate. "What else have you got?"

There was quite a variety all told. There were Heckler and Koch machine-pistols, revolvers and self-loading pistols, hand-grenades and a couple of Browning heavy machine-guns. In addition there was a large quantity of ammunition.

Grady was not the kind of man to show any great emotion, but it was apparent that he was pleased.

O'Higgins seemed to be expecting rather more reaction. "Are you happy?"

Grady looked at him. "Happy?"

"This is what you want, isn't it? All this hardware."

"Sure it's what we want," Grady said. "But we haven't got it yet, have we? I mean right now it's all here, isn't it? I won't be happy until it's in the hands that are needing it."

"But it will be. All in good time."

"If nothing goes wrong."

"If anything goes wrong it won't be at this end." O'Higgins spoke rather sharply. "What may happen after the stuff is transferred to the fishing-boat on the other side of the pond is another matter. It'll be out of our hands then and up to your boys to see that it gets ashore."

"So it will. And we'll do our best, have no fear on that score. But it only takes one little leak, one little word spoken in the wrong quarter, and what do we have? A shot across the bows and a boarding party of naval ratings or Customs Officers making a search from stem to stern."

O'Higgins frowned. "Are you suggesting there might be an informer?"

"It's happened before. It could happen again."

"It amazes me that you haven't got rid of that kind of poison from the organization long ago."

"If anyone would tell us an infallible way of doing so we'd be all ears," Grady said. "But it's not as easy as it sounds. And besides, in a situation such as this how would we know for sure which side of the Atlantic the whisper came from?"

"Now see here," McNulty chipped in. "Are you suggesting that one of us —"

"I'm suggesting nothing," Grady said. "I'm just putting the question."

"There's no traitors in our lot," McNulty said in a blustering tone. "What do you say, fellers?" He looked at the others, appealing for support.

There was a general murmur of denial, a hint of resentment that anyone should imagine such a possibility.

"It wouldn't have to be a traitor," Grady said softly. "Just a blabber-mouth; someone with the drink taken and the tongue loosened; boasting, getting some reflected glory from the brave boys across the sea who might be dying in their own red blood because of a careless word."

30

There was an uneasy silence when he stopped speaking. Fawley wondered whether the words had touched a sensitive spot here and there. One thing was certain: Grady did not hesitate to speak his mind; he was no servile beggar humbly grateful for any hand-out. Rather he seemed to take what was offered as if by right, as though he regarded it as a privilege for the Americans to dip into their well-lined pockets in support of the cause.

O'Higgins cleared his throat. "Well now, let's not get to bickering amongst ourselves. So maybe there has been some poor security in the past, right here as well as in the old country. But what's done is done and the thing is to make sure it doesn't happen again. Okay?"

The others mumbled something Which might have been taken as agreement, but Fawley sensed that the spirit of hearty good fellowship that had been there at the start had largely evaporated. The farewells as they left the warehouse and got into their cars were muted, and there could be no doubt at all that it was Grady who had brought about this dampening effect by his acidity. There was an abrasive quality about the little man and he made no attempt to be ingratiating.

"You want to take a look at the ship now?" O'Higgins asked.

"May as well," Grady said.

The others were turning their cars and driving away. Only Fawley and the two older men were left.

"Okay then," O'Higgins said. "Let's go."

It was berthed close by, a small freighter, rather venerable and of undistinguished aspect. Nothing much appeared to be doing on board, but they found the captain, who welcomed them to his cabin. His name was Brown and he had met O'Higgins before. O'Higgins introduced Grady and Fawley, and Brown shook hands with each of them. There was a raffish, buccaneering look about him; he was the sort of man you might have expected to run across in seedy bars and disreputable places of questionable entertainment in any port in the world from Rotterdam to Singapore, from Tangier to San Francisco; a man who would do almost anything for money and throw it away on a horse or a whore as soon as he had it.

Brown produced a bottle of Scotch and some glasses. O'Higgins and Grady accepted the offer of a drink but Fawley shook his head.

"Not for me, thanks."

"No?" Brown seemed amazed at the refusal.

"He's a wise man," O'Higgins said. "He never touches spirits and he doesn't smoke. He has too much concern for his health."

"Is that a fact?" The captain appeared to find it an odd obsession. "Me, I never give it a thought. Can't recall when I last went to a doctor."

"Maybe you should have a check-up."

"What, pay some guy to tell me I'll die if I don't give up all the things that make life worth living! No thanks. I'll die anyway when the time comes, but I'm not going to get ulcers worrying about it."

Grady was showing signs of impatience with this conversation. "We'll all die," he said. "The question is, do we die as free men or do we die in chains?"

Brown gazed at him with the faintest of faint smiles twitching his moist lips. "It's a good question certainly, but how in hades do you tell which is the free man and which the slave?"

Grady seemed ready to have a go at him over that but thought better of it.

O'Higgins suggested that they should get down to business. "Everything is in order, I take it, Captain?"

"As far as I'm concerned," Brown said, "yes. There's just a few more items of cargo to be taken aboard, which I don't need to describe to you gentlemen; then we'll be ready to sail."

"For the Azores?"

"Sure."

"But you'll not be going there direct, I think?" The question was superfluous. O'Higgins knew the answer.

"We'll be making no landfall before we reach the islands," Brown said, with studied innocence.

"No landfall, but a rendezvous perhaps?"

"As to that," Brown said, "I'm still waiting for the necessary information. I haven't been given the coordinates yet."

O'Higgins looked at Grady, who hesitated a moment or two as though reluctant to part with the information they all knew he possessed; but then he reached into an inner pocket and took out a sealed envelope. This he handed to Brown, who tore it open and removed a folded sheet of paper. There was no message written on the paper, just a few figures and letters.

"Good enough?" Grady asked.

"Good enough for me," Brown said. "Just so long as the boat turns up."

"You can count on that."

"I just hope I can. Because if it doesn't I'll dump the stuff overboard. I'm not going to hang around."

"You can't do that," Grady said sharply.

Brown was cool. "On board this ship," he said, "you'd be surprised what I can do."

O'Higgins broke in again, pouring oil on what gave signs of becoming troubled waters. "I'm sure it won't come to that. Everything will go fine, just fine."

They left soon after that. On the way back to the house on Riverside Drive, Grady said:

"Do you trust that man?"

"Now there's a question," O'Higgins said. "Why do you ask?"

"I think he's a crook."

"Well, sure he is. That's why we're dealing with him. Who else but a crook would be any use to us? Where would you find an honest sea captain with his own ship who'd be willing to do a bit of tampering with the paper-work? Where would you find a law-abiding ship's master prepared to take his vessel miles off course to make a rendezvous with a fishing-boat and transfer a consignment of Armalite rifles and Browning machine-guns and ammunition and God knows what which never should legally have been on board in the first place?"

Grady was silent.

"The fact is," O'Higgins said, "that for an operation of this kind you need not only a crooked captain but a crooked crew as well. And you don't get that sort of thing from one of the top class shipping lines; they wouldn't want to know."

Grady still appeared only half satisfied. "I'm not sure I should've given him the information. Maybe I should've held on to it for a while longer."

"And where would have been the sense in that, for God's sake?" O'Higgins sounded as if he were losing his patience. "He's got to know the latitude and longitude if he's to make the rendezvous; it stands to reason. And as I see it, it doesn't make a cent's worth of difference whether he has the information today or tomorrow or the day after. He's not going to broadcast it all around the town, because it's in his interests not to."

"Anyway," Grady said, "I didn't like what he said about throwing the stuff overboard if the fishing-boat didn't turn up."

"That was just talk. He didn't mean it."

"I think he did."

"Well, it won't ever come to that, will it? The boat's going to be there."

"There could be delays; you know the way things are; they don't always go strictly according to plan. Brown says he's not going to wait."

"He'll wait. He'll give it time. You'll see."

"I hope so; I surely hope so."

"You worry too much," O'Higgins said.

When they got back to the house, O'Higgins took Grady to the library for a heart-to-heart talk, while Fawley went to his own room. Later O'Higgins sent a request to his nephew to join him and the Irishman. Fawley went at once and found the two men waiting for him. O'Higgins, he thought, looked pretty pleased with himself, as though he had just brought off a successful business deal. Grady looked rather less pleased.

"Well, Clyde my boy," O'Higgins said, "it's all settled. Mr Grady is going to put in a word for you on the other side, and as soon as the message comes through you'll be on your way."

Fawley glanced at Grady. He guessed that O'Higgins had been doing some heavy persuasion and had extracted a somewhat unwilling agreement from his guest.

"It may not be as easy as all that," Grady said. "It won't be just a matter of my say-so. There's other people to take into account."

O'Higgins brushed aside the quibble. "Sure, sure. But I'll make a bet they'll see it our way when you've explained the situation. You scratch my back, I scratch yours. That's how it goes." He winked heavily. "And what do you have to lose?"

Fawley had some misgiving. It was obvious that O'Higgins had used the financial argument to break down Grady's resistance. But if Grady could be taken as an example of the Provisionals' reluctance to admit a so-called outsider to their ranks, and if they could only be persuaded to do so under extreme pressure, was it such a great idea after all? He had imagined in his innocence that a volunteer fighter for the cause would have been welcomed with enthusiasm, that one had only to offer oneself in order to be taken immediately and gratefully into the fold. But apparently it was not so; it seemed that they would be doing him a big favour just by letting him in. It was not quite as he would have wished it to be.

"Look, Mr Grady," he said, "if you don't really want me –"

"Want you! Of course he wants you," O'Higgins broke in. "What are you talking about?"

"It's hardly the impression I'm getting," Fawley said. "And I don't want to push myself in where I'm not welcome. I'd rather not go at all."

O'Higgins stared at him. "Here, what is this? Don't tell me you're getting cold feet."

"It's not a question of cold feet. It's all a question of whether or not they want volunteers. I get the feeling they don't. And if not, well, that's it, isn't it?"

O'Higgins turned to Grady. "Tell him."

"I think they'll want you," Grady said.

"And you'll give your recommendation?"

"I'll give my recommendation."

"Sure, you will," O'Higgins said. "And there won't be any trouble."

"I hope not," Grady said. "I don't think there will."

O'Higgins turned again to Fawley. "You see? Now let's have no more talk of pulling out. Everything's going to be okay. Right?"

"Right," Fawley said.

But he would have liked to see a bit more enthusiasm on Grady's part and less evidence that he was only agreeing to the arrangement because he had been pressured into it. Somehow, it was all rather unsatisfactory. But maybe it would turn out all right.

Chapter Five – ONE TOO MANY

Events moved more swiftly than Fawley had anticipated. He had had a feeling that Grady might drag his feet or that there would be opposition from other people. Grady's obvious lack of enthusiasm for the business had had a depressing effect and he was no longer so sanguine in his expectations as he had been before the meeting with the Irishman.

As things turned out, however, he had to wait very little time before receiving the call. Unenthusiastic though Grady might have seemed, it was evident that he had carried out his promise with expedition.

"You see," O'Higgins said. "They do want you. I knew they would."

Fawley still wondered whether it was really him they wanted and not just the financial and other aid which a refusal might have put in jeopardy, but he said nothing.

"You're all ready to go?" O'Higgins asked.

"I'm ready," Fawley said.

A few days later he was in Dublin. He had been given the address of a modest hotel and he took a room and waited for someone to make contact with him. Two days passed and nothing had happened. He wondered whether he was expected to hang around at the hotel, but he felt that to do so might have made him conspicuous and he had a desire to see something of this city which he had dreamed about from the days of childhood. So he went out.

He found O'Connell Street and Parnell Square, named after those heroes of Ireland's struggle who had figured so often in his Uncle Danny's stories. He stood on a bridge and watched the Liffey flowing past; it was smaller and dirtier than he had imagined it, but it thrilled him nonetheless to see it so close at hand. He dropped a coin in it – for luck.

The mere fact of being in Ireland made his heart beat faster; and yet it seemed to him that the people of Dublin were oddly calm and unconcerned, going about their daily business as quietly as if there had been no life-and-death struggle going on for the freedom of the north. It was almost as if they did not care; as though the fate of their Catholic brethren in Ulster was none of their business.

But perhaps this was a false impression; perhaps beneath the apparent impassivity was a burning passion for the unification of their beloved country and the expulsion of the hated British from their shores. It had to be so; it was inconceivable that it should be otherwise; he could not believe that they simply did not care.

On the third day he was contacted by a man named Ryan, a short plump individual with an engaging grin and a twinkle in his eye.

"So you're our Mr Fawley," Ryan said; and he gave Fawley a curious sidelong glance, as though making a rapid mental assessment of what he saw. "You're the young American as is going to show us all the way we ought to go."

"Oh, I wouldn't say that," Fawley protested. He saw that Ryan was laughing at him in a gently mocking way. "I just want to help, that's all."

"Sure you do. And all credit to you for it. A mite of help is worth a deal of pity any day of the week."

"So you do want me?"

"Want you!" Ryan appeared astonished that such a question should be asked. "Why wouldn't we be wanting you, for mercy's sake?"

"I don't know. It just occurred to me that perhaps outsiders might not be welcome."

"What made you think that?"

"It was an impression I got from one of your people I met in America."

"Ah now," Ryan said. "Don't be taking any notice of that. Some people is very cautious."

"So it's not true?"

"Never a bit of it. You're as welcome as the flowers in spring, so y'are."

"Well, I'm glad to hear it. I wouldn't want to push myself in where I wasn't wanted."

"No fear of that," Ryan said. "Let's go and have a drink and a bit of talk."

He took Fawley to an old-fashioned public-house, full of mirrors and mahogany and marble-topped tables, where he introduced the young man to a dark liquid with a thick lid of froth on top. Fawley learned that the liquid was called Guinness. He had never tasted it before and he was not at all sure he liked it; in fact he was pretty certain he did not. Ryan swallowed his first half-pint with scarcely a pause for breath, and Fawley bought him another. After that he bought several more for the tubby little man, who appeared to have a great capacity for the dark liquid; but he made the one glass suffice for himself. Ryan seemed to be quite happy with this arrangement.

"You'll not be a heavy drinker, Mr Fawley?"

"I hardly ever touch alcohol," Fawley admitted.

"It's a poison, so they say." Ryan took another swallow. "Ah well, we all have to die sometime," he added philosophically, "and it's a nice way to go." He regarded Fawley thoughtfully. "It's a question of deciding where you'll best fit in. You'd like to see some action, would you not?"

"Yes."

"So it's not a desk job you'll be wanting? No. Well, we don't have such a lot of them anyway. Active service, is it?"

"Yes."

"Are you good with guns?"

"Pretty good."

"And explosives?"

Fawley shook his head. "I've had no experience with that sort of material."

"Have you not? There's a pity. Still, it's no matter. We have lads that are dab hands at the bomb-making, so we have."

"When do you think I'll be given a job?" Fawley asked.

Ryan gave a grin. "Eager to get started, is it?"

"It's what I'm here for. And I've come a long way."

"So you have; there's no denying that. But don't be getting impatient. Give it time. We'll keep in touch."

Fawley had to be content with that. He was not at all satisfied with the situation; the days passed and nothing seemed to be moving as far as he was concerned. Now and then Ryan turned up and took him to various public-houses where he drank Guinness at Fawley's expense and talked of this and that. But he never introduced the American to any other members of the IRA and was evasive when pressed on this subject.

"They're busy men; they have a lot to do. You're maybe thinking it's time you was doing something, time you was given an assignment, a mission or some such?"

"Well, I'm not doing much good just killing time."

"Sure y'are. It's acclimatizing yourself you need to be doing; getting the feel of things. Isn't that so?"

Fawley wondered just what things he was supposed to be getting the feel of. He had a suspicion that he was being given the run-around. Maybe they didn't trust him; maybe Ryan had been deputed to fob him off with half-promises, keeping him quiet until perhaps he lost his enthusiasm and decided to go back to the States. Even about himself Ryan gave very little away. Fawley had no idea where he lived and had no means of getting in touch with him; it was left entirely to Ryan to make contact when he felt like doing so. And for all that resulted from these contacts they might as well not have been made.

Sometimes he wondered whether Ryan was a genuine IRA man. He was not Fawley's idea of a patriot or freedom fighter; his chief interest seemed to lie in drinking Guinness and his talk was mostly of matters that had nothing whatever to do with the deadly business that was going on north of the border. So maybe he was just a go-between employed by the IRA, a hanger-on, a nobody. But the fact remained that, whoever he might be, he was the only link Fawley had with the people he had come to join.

One day Ryan turned up with a copy of the *Irish Times*, which contained a report of a car-bomb explosion in a small town in Armagh. There were pictures of the devastation that had been caused.

"The boys have been busy, you see," Ryan said, with evident satisfaction.

Fawley read the report. Six people had been killed and thirty injured, including ten women and two small children. No British soldiers or members of the Royal Ulster Constabulary appeared to have been involved. The Provisional IRA had claimed responsibility for the incident.

It was the first time that Fawley had been quite so close to an operation of the Provos. He was not exactly on the spot now, but there was a great difference between being less than a hundred miles from the scene and being three thousand miles away on the other side of the Atlantic Ocean. The impact was stronger and he was surprised by the mixed nature of his own reaction. Here in Ireland the issue seemed for the first time to be not quite so clearly defined in black and white. He could not avoid a feeling of distaste for Ryan's undisguised gloating.

"Will you look at the damage to them buildings! It must have been one lovely bomb, so it must."

"There were people killed," Fawley said.

"To be sure. That's what it's all about."

"But they were all civilians."

Ryan shrugged. "In this war there are no civilians. Only targets."

"And that includes children?"

"If the kids get in the way," Ryan said, "that's just too bad."

Two days later Fawley read about the shooting of a man of thirty-five as he was leaving a church in Belfast after attending Mass. His wife and two young children, a boy and a girl, were with him when the gunman walked up, put four bullets in his chest and made a get-away on the pillion of a motor-cycle. Again the Provisional IRA claimed responsibility.

Fawley was puzzled and he turned to Ryan for enlightenment.

"Why would they do that? He was a Catholic."

"Maybe he was," Ryan said. "But he was also a UDR man."

"UDR?"

"Ulster Defence Regiment. They're as bad as the Tommies and the constabulary."

Fawley saw that he still had much to learn about the conflict; there were aspects of it about which he had been ignorant in far-away America. It now appeared that the demarcation lines could be blurred; that there were bad Catholics as well as good ones. The good Catholics might be murdered by Loyalist gunmen while the bad ones were executed by the IRA.

He wondered whether Uncle Danny was aware of the confusion; he had certainly never mentioned it. Just as he had never mentioned the great mass of moderate people of both persuasions who wanted only peace and justice in Northern Ireland, an end to the killing and destruction which had been going on for so long that there were young men and women in Belfast and Derry and Portadown who could remember no other way of life.

He wondered what Ryan did for a living. Perhaps he was unemployed and could devote all his time to working for the IRA. He was always cheerful and friendly, but Fawley was not sure he really liked the man. And he did not altogether trust Ryan; he suspected a certain lack of frankness in him, although he always tried to give the impression that no one could have been more open and honest than he. The fact was that after more than a week in Dublin, Fawley had still not come face to face with any other member of the IRA and had received no information regarding his own future.

It was not what he had expected. He had imagined that as soon as he arrived in Ireland he would be taken to some officer of high rank in the organization, that he would be officially welcomed and that perhaps some ceremony of swearing in would take place. He realized, of course, that the IRA was not quite like any other army; it was a clandestine force, illegal even in the Republic, and must of necessity act with stealth; but surely there had to be accepted methods by which a volunteer could be absorbed into the ranks. And however hard he tried he could not see how such absorption was advanced by providing Ryan with an endless supply of free Guinness.

As the days passed he had an increasing sense of frustration. What was he doing? Why was he there? There seemed to be no point in it. He was almost at the end of his patience and seriously thinking of calling the whole thing off and returning to the States when Ryan turned up with a piece of information which put this idea out of his mind.

"Well," Ryan said, "they've finally decided what to do with you."

"Ah!" Fawley said, and waited to hear more.

"You're to go to London."

"London!" Fawley suspected Ryan of kidding, though he appeared quite serious. "What am I to go there for?"

"You'll be joining an active service unit. It's what you want, isn't it? Action."

"Yes, but I thought–"

"You thought it would be in Ireland? Sure you did. But the business doesn't all get done over here. There's other targets. We've operated on the Continent – Germany – anywhere the Tommies are. They never know when they're going to be hit."

"Yes, I realize that, but–"

"What's up?" Ryan asked. "Don't you want to go to London?"

If he had been perfectly honest Fawley might have replied that he did not. It was not the same as operating in Ireland; somehow for him it lacked the glamour; it was too far away from the centre of activity, from the country where the real struggle was taking place. But he had offered his services to the cause and he supposed he could hardly expect to pick and choose what job he did.

"I'll go wherever I'm told to go," he said.

"That's the spirit," Ryan said. He gave Fawley a pat on the shoulder. "Never say die."

"When am I to go?"

"In a day or two. Just as soon as arrangements can be made. Thought I'd give you the tip so you'd be at the ready."

"I've been at the ready ever since I came here."

"Fine, fine. Ever been to London?"

"No."

"Ah, then you'll be having a grand time of it, seeing the sights and all."

"I didn't think I was going there to see the sights."

"Not entirely, no. But there'll be the spare time and you'll be wanting to relax. There's no law that says you mustn't enjoy yourself once in a while, is there?"

"I guess not."

Ryan gave Fawley a quirky look. "Y'know what it is, Clyde old son; you take life too seriously. That's the way people go crazy. You should try to laugh a bit more; laughter's good for the soul."

"I don't see that there's so much to laugh about," Fawley said. "When I look around me it seems there's more reason for tears than laughter."

Ryan gave a shake of the head. "Ah now, you shouldn't take it to heart so. You can't be bearing all the world's troubles on your own two shoulders. But there, when all's said and done who am I to be telling you what to do? It's your life."

"Yes," Fawley said, "it is, isn't it?"

*

He travelled to London by way of Amsterdam, following instructions that had been given to him. Ryan explained that he was unlikely to be scrutinized so closely coming in from the Continent as he might have been if he had made the journey direct from Dublin. Fawley did not question the wisdom of this. He had very little luggage and nothing to declare.

He got a taxi at the airport and had himself taken to a small private hotel which Ryan had recommended. It was in the Hammersmith area and seemed to have little in its favour except a rather dingy anonymity. Here he was able to obtain a room, and having thus established his new base he took stock of the situation.

There was little in it to attract him. That part of London in which the hotel, or boarding-house as it might more accurately have been described, was situated seemed to be entirely without interest; if he had made a systematic search he doubted whether he could have found any place less remote from the struggle in which he had hoped to become engaged. It was as though he had been deliberately shunted off the main line into this unimportant siding where he would be safely out of the way and cause no bother to anyone. Could that really have been the object of the exercise? Had he in fact been sent here merely because he might have made a nuisance of himself in Ireland? He did not wish to believe it but it certainly appeared to be a possibility.

Well, perhaps tomorrow would provide an answer.

*

Ryan had given him the address and with the help of a street map and an inquiry or two he was able to find it. Not that it looked very much worth the effort when he had done so.

It was a jobbing builder's yard, rather cramped for room, as though it had only with difficulty managed to squeeze into the space between the buildings on each side. There was a pair of wooden doors on rusty hinges which gave access to the yard, and a painted sign on one post revealed the fact that the establishment operated under the trade name of DeeCee Repairers.

One of the doors was standing open and Fawley could see a rather battered pick-up truck on the left, some heaps of sand and shingle, a couple of ladders, a cement-mixer, a pile of timber and various other items essential to the building trade. On the right was an open shed and the back door of a three-storey house.

He walked into the yard and gazed around with some curiosity. What he saw hardly gave the impression that DeeCee Repairers was a particularly thriving concern. There was a drab, down-at-heel look about the place; even the timber appeared to consist chiefly of salvaged boards, pockmarked with holes from which the rusting nails had been withdrawn. Nothing looked new except the sand, and even that had been used by predatory cats as a convenient lavatory.

There was no activity in the yard, and the only moving thing in sight was a skinny nondescript sort of dog which was nosing around in the junk, apparently in the forlorn hope of discovering something edible.

Fawley looked at the truck, looked at the dog, looked at the house, and came to the conclusion that he had better go and knock on the door. He had taken only two steps towards it when it opened and a man came out.

The man spotted Fawley and came to a halt, eyeing him suspiciously. He was a chunky individual wearing jeans and a check shirt with the sleeves rolled up. He had thick forearms and black hair and a beard, and there was a mat of hair visible in the opening of the shirt where a small silver cross, suspended from a chain around his neck, nestled snugly in the undergrowth. His nose was like a blob of putty that had been stuck on to the face as a kind of afterthought, and he had no discernible forehead because the black tresses above came down to join forces with a pair of bristling eyebrows below. Indeed, the proportion of his features that was visible to the beholder was so limited by the encroaching growth all round that it was impossible to tell just what he would have looked like without it.

On seeing the man Fawley had also come to a halt, and the two of them stood for a while gazing warily at each other from a distance of some fifteen yards or so. It was the man who was first to speak, and he did so in the accent which Fawley had become accustomed to in the past week or two, though his ear was not yet so well attuned to it that he could distinguish the brogue of one part of Ireland from that of another.

"Would you be looking for someone?" the man asked.

"Yes," Fawley said. "A man named Duggan."

"And what makes you think you'll be finding him here, will you tell me?"

"I was told to come to this address. My name is Fawley."

"Oh, it is, is it?" The man advanced a few paces as if to take a closer look at Fawley. "And who might it have been who told you that?"

"A man named Ryan. In Dublin."

"Dublin, is it?" The man scratched his right cheek, as though an itch had developed under the covering of dark hair. "Now there's a fine old city to be sure. What do you say, Mr Fawley?"

"I say it's a fine old city."

"You was there long?"

"A week or two."

"And then you was sent here?"

"Yes. Weren't you warned I'd be coming?"

The bearded man did not answer the question. He said gruffly: "You'd better step inside." Then he turned abruptly and walked towards the door of the house.

Fawley went with him.

The door opened into a kitchen which might have benefited from a thorough clean-up. There was a lingering odour of fried bacon and damp dishcloth. In the sink was a litter of dirty china and cutlery waiting for someone to make an attack on it.

The bearded man led the way through the kitchen and into an ill-lighted hall. He opened a door on the right and conducted Fawley into a room that appeared to have been turned into an office. There were two or three chairs and a dented metal filing cabinet and an old iron safe standing in one corner. A large wicker wastepaper basket was full to overflowing with screwed up balls of paper and there was an open fireplace in which were some dead ashes that looked as though they might have lain there for months. The floorboards were bare and exhibited the evidence of worm in them, and there was an old-fashioned roll-top desk pushed up against one wall.

A man was sitting at the desk and pecking at a typewriter with two fingers. He stopped when the bearded man brought Fawley in, turned in his chair and stared at them. He was slightly-built, thin-faced and clean-shaven, his brown hair cropped very short. The immediate impression that Fawley got was that here was a real hard character; it showed in the eyes, which were lacking in all warmth, and in the general aspect of the man. He looked as tough as old leather.

"What have we here?" he asked.

The bearded man answered. "Says his name's Fawley. Says he was sent from Dublin by somebody named Ryan. Says he was told to contact a man named Duggan."

The man at the desk probed Fawley with his chilling eyes. "Is that so?"

"It's so."

"I'm Duggan," the man said.

Fawley had already guessed as much. This was the man he had been told to report to, the man from whom he would now take his orders. He looked at Duggan and had misgivings. This was not the kind of man he would have chosen to work with if he had had any say in the matter. But there was nothing he could do about it; he had either to accept the situation as it was or pull out and go home. And if he went home what would he say to Uncle Danny? That he had not liked the company? That things had not turned out quite as he would have wished, and so he had no more taste for the venture? He could imagine O'Higgins's reaction to that argument. No, he could not pull out; he had to go on with it.

"You know why I'm here?" he asked.

"Oh, we know. You're here because you've been planted on us by them that order these things. We've had instructions to take you in hand. We're to use you, God help us, whether we like it or not. We don't have any choice."

"You don't seem very happy about it."

"Happy! Why should I be happy? I'll be straight with you, Mr Fawley; the last thing I want is to make myself responsible for a bloody amateur."

"Is that what you think I am?"

"What else? Oh, I know you probably see yourself as some kind of knight in shining armour come all the way from America to give us poor useless bastards a helping hand. But in my book you're still an amateur and maybe a liability."

"I'm sorry you see it in that way," Fawley said. "Maybe you'd rather I gave up the idea and went away?"

"You bet your sweet life I'd rather you did. But it's not on, is it? I have to obey orders, else I'm in trouble. And my orders are to use you. That's all there is to it."

The bearded man put in a question. "What can you do, pal?"

"I can use a gun," Fawley said. He could think of nothing else that might impress them.

Duggan received the information with no evidence of joy. "Oh, fine. So we can send you out on the streets to shoot a few Brits. Is that the idea?"

Put like that it sounded just plain stupid and Fawley was silent.

"Well," Duggan said, "I suppose we'll have to think of something." He spoke to the bearded man. "Does he know your name?"

"No."

Duggan turned to Fawley. "He's Sean Connolly. You'd better be nice to him because he could break your arm if he had a grudge against you."

"I hope that won't be necessary," Fawley said. He was not sure whether it had been meant as a joke or had been a serious warning. He thought Connolly looked capable of breaking an arm if he felt like it.

He heard someone come into the house, and a moment later the door of the room opened and a girl walked in. She might have been about twenty-five years old and she was wearing faded cord trousers and a black turtle-neck jumper. She was fairly tall and had dark brown hair which was in a mess and a figure which certainly was not; the cords fitted so tightly they might have been made on her and she was as slim as a lath.

She came to a halt just inside the room and stared at Fawley, and he reflected that she might have been quite a beauty if she had taken any trouble with her appearance; but seemed not to give a damn about it. When she had taken a good look at Fawley she turned to Duggan.

"Is this him?" she asked.

"It's him," Duggan said. "Mr Fawley, our new recruit, all ready and eager to get his teeth into something, even if he doesn't know what." He spoke with a kind of sneer and then added for Fawley's benefit, "This is Molly. Now you've met the lot of us; there's nobody else."

46

It was a cell; just the three of them; a self-contained unit formed to work on its own and having no direct links with any other cell but taking its orders only from the top. Now, with the arrival of Fawley, the cell had expanded to four. And perhaps to the original three that looked like one too many.

Chapter Six – NO GOING BACK

It was Duggan who suggested, and indeed insisted, that Fawley should leave the hotel and move into a bed-sitter. He said that Fawley's comings and goings would be less conspicuous in such surroundings. It was he who directed the young American to Raven House which was within easy reach of the builder's yard.

Fawley made no objections; it was not the style of accommodation to which he had been accustomed in his uncle's New York house, but he regarded himself as being now on active service and a certain roughness in living conditions was only to be expected.

Duggan also supplied the Browning pistol, though he questioned the need for it. "Why do you want a gun? You'll be better off without one."

But Fawley disagreed; he felt that a gun would be a kind of symbol, something with which to convince himself that he did really belong to the organization, the Irish Republican Army. For there had been precious little proof of that so far; no enrolment ceremony or anything of that description; and contact only with a man named Ryan and the cell at the premises of a firm called DeeCee Repairers. It was not much; it really was not much at all.

In the end Duggan yielded to persuasion and came up with the Browning, but he made Fawley pay for it. Fawley thought the price was rather steep, but he was not short of money and he paid up without a quibble.

The morning after he moved into the room at Raven House Fawley paid another visit to the DeeCee Repairers' place of business. It was getting on for ten o'clock, but he found the two men and the girl eating breakfast in the kitchen of the house.

"What do you want?" Duggan said.

"I just thought I'd better report in."

Duggan treated him to a bleak stare. "Why?"

"In case there was something you wanted me to do."

"Like what?"

"I don't know. I –"

"Can you lay bricks? Can you paint? Can you plaster a ceiling?"

Connolly gave a laugh and Fawley reddened; he did not take kindly to being ridiculed. The girl was regarding him with a faintly contemptuous expression.

"I wasn't thinking of anything in the building and decorating line," he said.

"No?" Duggan raised an eyebrow. "Maybe you thought we'd have a bit of bombing for you, or a piece of sniping perhaps; some little job like that just to get your hand in. Is that it?"

"Well, I –"

"Forget it. I don't know what stupid ideas you've got in your head about the way we work, but I can tell you it's not all go, go, go. There's planning, there's reconnaissance, there's just plain waiting until the time is right. D'you understand what I'm saying?"

"I understand," Fawley said. "But if I'm to be any use I'll need to keep in touch, won't I?"

"You don't have to keep in touch with us; we'll be in touch with you. If anything comes up we'll let you know. But we don't want you hanging round here all the time. That way you could get yourself noticed and some people might begin to wonder what sort of business was bringing you here day after day. You get my point?"

"I get it."

Fawley was chastened. He felt foolish. His eagerness to help, to be doing something, appeared more than a little ridiculous when confronted by the phlegmatic down-to-earth calm of the two men and the girl.

"Have you had breakfast?" Molly asked.

"I don't eat breakfast," Fawley said.

"You don't?" She seemed astonished by this revelation. "Maybe you could drink a cup of tea?"

Fawley had no desire for tea, but he accepted the offer, since it was the first conciliatory gesture that had come from any one of them and he did not wish to give offence by rejecting it. The tea was poured from a large brown pot into a cracked mug; it was dark and sweet and strong and he hated it; but he drank it nevertheless.

When he left the house Molly was making a reluctant start on the arrears of washing-up, a cigarette between her lips shedding ash in the water. He wondered which of the men she slept with, but it was not a question he would have dared to ask. Judging by the look of the place, she was no enthusiast for the science of domestic economy.

*

When Fawley returned to Raven House he was waylaid on the first-floor landing by an elderly lady who introduced herself as Miss Flora Wills.

"You're Mr Fawley, aren't you?"

Fawley admitted the fact.

"And an American, too?"

"Yes."

"I heard you'd moved in. So nice to have a young man in the house. And an American. I was in New York, oh, years ago. On the stage, you know. I was a dancer."

Fawley gave Miss Wills a closer look and found it hard to believe. But it was possible of course; even dancers grew old and shrivelled and perhaps a trifle unsteady on their legs, as this one appeared to be. Miss Wills had white hair and a face like an apple that had endured a winter on the shelf; she herself had probably been on the shelf for a good many winters, though it was still possible to detect a lingering hint or two of the pretty girl she might have been when young.

"I'm on the next floor," Miss Wills said. "Would you care to come up and see my room?"

"Well, I'm not sure I –"

"Oh, do, please. Just for a minute or two. We can get to know each other better."

Fawley was not at all sure he wanted to know Miss Wills any better; but she was very pressing and he guessed that she was lonely and glad to have anyone to talk to. So, against his better judgement, he allowed himself to be persuaded.

The room was so cluttered with furniture and knick-knacks that it was difficult to move around in it without knocking something over. Miss Wills appeared to have gathered mementoes from everywhere she had been, and it was evident that she had been to a great many places in her time. The minute or two seemed to stretch out to indefinite length as Miss Wills, having succeeded in luring Fawley into her little nest, proceeded to give him the run-down of her life.

She had apparently been in the chorus line of a considerable number of musical shows which Fawley had never heard of. She made him sit in a worn but comfortable armchair while she showed him files of ancient press-cuttings and albums of photographs wherein she appeared as a sweet young thing in the fashions of the twenties and thirties. She spoke of C.B.

Cochran and André Chariot and the Littlers, who were mere names to Fawley and meant nothing to him; and whenever he made an attempt to leave she urged him to stay just a few more minutes because it was so nice to have someone who would listen to an old woman's chatter.

"People don't have much time for you when you've lived as long as I have. They think you're just a cranky old bore. I hope you don't think that."

"Why no," Fawley said. He felt sorry for Miss Wills; it must have been hard for her living alone in a miserable bed-sitter with only her memories of a very different kind of existence to sustain her. He rather liked the old girl, too, and he guessed that she was having to manage on a pretty meagre income. "You must have had an interesting career on the stage."

"It had its moments," Miss Wills confessed. "You're probably wondering why I never married."

"I'm sure it wasn't for lack of opportunity."

"That's true. There were so many young men; I could have had my pick. But somehow it never happened. And now –" Miss Wills sounded wistful. She gave a sigh. "Well, you can't turn the clock back, can you?"

"I guess not."

He got away at last. Miss Wills came to the door with him. "It's been so nice meeting you, Mr Fawley. We must have another little chat sometime. You're always most welcome."

"Well, thanks," Fawley said.

Miss Wills pointed at a door on the other side of the landing. "That's Mr Creech's room. Have you met him?"

"No."

"You will. He'll probably ask you to lend him money. Don't. He's not a very respectable person."

"I'll bear that in mind," Fawley said.

He had not been back in his own room for more than a few minutes when there was a knock on the door, and when he opened it he found a thin gaunt man standing outside.

"Creech," the man said. "Arthur Creech. I'm on the floor above. Thought I'd call and make your acquaintance, Mr Fawley. Mind if I come in?"

"Well –" Fawley said; but Creech was already in the room and it was too late to shut the door in his face.

"You're American, I hear," Creech said. He had greasy receding hair, a sharply pointed nose and prominent teeth. "Got a job over here or just staying temp'ry like?"

"I don't have a job," Fawley said. "I'm gathering material for a book."

"Ah! A littery gent. Studying the natives, that sort of thing. Very nice." As he talked Creech was giving Fawley and the room a close inspection with his beady close-set eyes, his gaze constantly shifting from one point to another. "You wouldn't have a drop of whisky or something of that sort, would you?"

"I'm afraid not."

"Ah, well! Not to worry." Mr Creech sat himself down in one of the chairs. "I'm a man of business myself."

"Oh!" Fawley said. Judging from his visitor's appearance, which was shabby to say the least, he would have guessed that it was not a particularly thriving business. But if it had been it was unlikely that Creech would have been residing in Raven House; unless he was very eccentric.

"Mail order. That line of country."

Fawley wondered what kind of goods Creech sold by mail order and where he kept his stock. Perhaps he had a warehouse somewhere; but it seemed unlikely.

"It's a growth industry," Creech said. "A man who was looking for a good investment could do worse than put his money in mail order. Take yourself, Mr Fawley; I don't know how you're fixed moneywise, but if you've got a few quid lying around and doing nothing – or should I say dollars? – I could guarantee a return of a minimum of fifty per cent per annum."

"Invested in your business?"

"Invested in my business. You couldn't do better."

Fawley was amazed at Creech's audacity. It was a con of course, and a pretty crude one at that. But he doubted whether Creech himself had any expectation of its succeeding. Maybe he was just trying it on for the hell of it.

"Well, thanks for the offer," Fawley said, "but I don't have a great deal of money, and what there is is all tied up right now. You know how it is."

Creech nodded. "I know." He did not appear at all disappointed; his expectations had obviously been low. "Anyway, the offer's there. Just keep it in mind."

"I'll do that," Fawley said.

Just as he was leaving Creech turned in the doorway and said: "By the way, I suppose you couldn't lend me ten quid, could you? Pounds, that is. I find myself a bit short of the ready. Let you have it back next week without fail."

Fawley remembered Miss Wills's warning. "Now there's an odd thing," he said. "I happen to be fresh out of cash myself. Sorry."

Creech gave him a look which said quite plainly that he did not believe a word of it. "Well," he said, "I shall just have to raid the gas meter, shan't I?"

*

It was the next morning when a freckle-faced boy delivered a note sealed in an unaddressed envelope. He knocked on the door of the room and when Fawley opened it he said:

"Are you Mr Fawley?"

"I am," Fawley said.

"This is for you, then," the boy said, and he handed over the envelope and started moving away.

Fawley stopped him. "Wait a moment. Who gave you this?"

The boy halted. "A man."

"What man?"

"He didn't give no name. He said you'd know."

"Okay," Fawley said. He could make a guess at the identity of the sender of the missive, and when he had opened the envelope and read the note he was sure the guess had been correct.

The note was written in block capitals. It was brief and it was unsigned. It read: "Come this morning".

He had nothing better to do, so he went at once. Connolly was in the yard doing some work on a Ford Cortina, a rather dingy grey car that had seen better days. He saw Fawley and walked across to him, wiping his hands on a cleaning-rag.

"So you got the message?"

"I got it. What's this all about?"

"Let's go inside and you'll hear."

He led the way into the house and they found Duggan and Molly in the office. Duggan came straight to the point.

"We've got a job for you."

Fawley's pulse quickened. So things were moving; he had not had to wait very long after all; they were ready to use him.

"What sort of job?"

"We're going to raid a post office and we've decided to take you along. It'll be experience for you."

Fawley stared at him in disbelief. "Raid a post office! Why? What for?" He could see no way in which such an operation could further the cause of Irish freedom.

"For the cash," Duggan said. "What else?"

"You're talking about a robbery?" It sounded incredible. There had to be some mistake.

"You can call it that if you like."

"But that's a crime."

Connolly gave a contemptuous laugh. "Crime, he says! And isn't it a crime the Brits are committin' in Ulster every blessed day of the week!"

"But why?" Fawley said. "Why is it necessary to rob a post office? I don't understand."

"The reason's simple," Duggan said. "We need the money. We have expenses, you know."

"But you have the business."

"Business!" Molly said. "That's a laugh."

"Be your age," Duggan said. "Don't you see the business is nothing but a front? We have to have a cover, else we'd rouse suspicion and the coppers might get ideas."

"Are you telling me you don't do any building or work of that kind?"

"Oh, we do a job here and there to keep up appearances, but it's not enough to pay the expenses. We never intended it should be. It's good camouflage, though."

"Don't you get any funds from the organization?"

"They need all the funds they can get themselves, over on the other side. Why would they be throwing good money away on the likes of us when we can get our own?"

Fawley was silent. This was a development he had never expected; it had never occurred to him that giving his services to the IRA might involve him in such criminal operations as common robbery. There was not much glamour about that.

"I believe our Clyde's unhappy about it," Molly said. "I told you he wouldn't like it."

"Don't you like it, Clyde?" Duggan asked.

Fawley shook his head. "It's not quite what I thought I was volunteering for. This will put me in the same category as thieves and muggers; people like that."

"It will not," Duggan said.

"So what's the difference?"

"The difference is that we're not doing this for personal gain; we're fighting a war; a holy war, you might call it. We're soldiers operating behind enemy lines and we're entitled to live off the land. This is no gentlemen's contest; this is a free for all with no holds barred. So are you with us or are you not? Because if you aren't you'd better walk out here and now. And don't imagine you can stay in and just do the jobs that happen to appeal to you; that's not on; it's all or nothing. So what's it to be, Clyde? In or out?"

Fawley hesitated. They were all watching him, waiting for his answer; and it occurred to him to wonder what they would do if he said he was out. Would they simply let him walk away, knowing what he did about them? He doubted it. They would never feel safe.

But it made no difference; he would not have walked out anyway; after coming so far he could not draw back now; he had to go on.

"Count me in," he said.

He had been aware of a certain tension building up, but now they all seemed to relax and the tension evaporated. Molly smiled at him. Connolly grinned.

"That's the boy," Duggan said. "And it won't be so bad; you'll see."

Fawley doubted it. He had grave misgivings. He saw now that he had let himself in for something he could never have anticipated and never would have believed possible. And he did not like it, did not like it at all. But it had to be. There could be no going back now.

Chapter Seven – WITH VIOLENCE

It was in Buckinghamshire, a fairly large village with a couple of public-houses and a church with a square stone tower and a leaded roof. There was not a sign of life anywhere when they arrived at about one o'clock in the morning; all the houses were dark and silent and there was not even a dog barking.

Connolly was driving. It was not the Cortina; Duggan and Molly and Fawley had travelled the first part of the journey in that car before switching to the Vauxhall Cavalier which Connolly had stolen earlier in the day. He had been waiting for them at a prearranged rendezvous and they had left the Cortina there to pick up on the way back.

It was all new territory to Fawley and he had hardly the vaguest notion of where he was being taken. Not that it would have been any advantage to him if he had known; he felt like a twig or a dead leaf being carried along by a stream and powerless to resist the current that had him in its grip.

He was carrying the gun, the Browning pistol that he had bought from Duggan, but he hoped there would be no occasion to use it. There was a flutter in his stomach, a feeling of excitement such as he had experienced on his first hunting trip, not knowing quite what was in store for him. But there had been a sense of joy then, a keen delight in the adventure; now there was no joy and no delight, only a sick nervous apprehension.

The post office was a red-brick building standing well back from the road, with a gravelled forecourt at the edge of which a pillar-box stood in splendid isolation like a devoted sentry keeping watch in the night. A street-lamp not far away bathed the building in a wash of rosy light, but from the place itself there came no indication that anyone inside was awake or moving.

Connolly stopped the car at the side of the road some twenty yards or so from the post office and switched off the headlights.

"Right," Duggan said. "Get the masks on."

The masks were balaclava helmets. Duggan, Fawley and the girl put their helmets on and pushed their hands into rubber gloves. When they got out of the car Connolly remained in the driving-seat, ready for a quick get-away when the job had been completed. Duggan was carrying a canvas hold-all with a zip-fastener. Fawley could feel the hard bulge of the gun in his pocket. He was not sure whether or not the other two men were armed, but he suspected that Duggan at least had some kind of lethal weapon concealed about his person. Probably the girl had one also.

They quickly crossed the forecourt with Duggan in the lead. It was obvious that he had been there before and knew his way around. He pushed open a gate at one side of the building which gave access to a yard at the rear and the other two followed him in. They were now out of sight from anyone who might pass by on the road and Fawley breathed more easily, though his pulse was still beating at a faster rate than was normal.

Although they were now away from the light of the street-lamp there was enough moonlight to reveal the back door of the post office, and it was to this that Duggan turned his attention. He put the hold-all on the ground and took from it a small iron crowbar or jemmy. This he inserted in the crevice between the door and the jamb and put some pressure on it. The door creaked but did not open. Duggan increased the pressure, but though the door again complained audibly it still held firm.

Duggan cursed softly. "Give's a hand, Clyde. Don't just stand there doing damn all."

Fawley thought it was crazy. Suppose there was a burglar alarm waiting to go off as soon as the door was opened. What then? Would Duggan call it off and beat a smart retreat or would he press on regardless? He was probably mad enough to do even that.

But when, under the weight of the two men, the door finally gave way with a sudden splintering of wood there came no sound of any alarm. Duggan put the jemmy back in the hold-all and took out an electric torch. He picked up the hold-all and with a curt order to Fawley to follow him walked into the house.

Fawley hesitated, but having come so far he felt impelled to go through with it. He too went inside and Molly followed, closing the door behind her. Duggan switched on the torch, revealing that they were in a short passageway with an archway on the right giving access to a staircase. A door on the left opened into what appeared to be a kitchen, but straight ahead was the public part of the building and with Duggan still leading the way they came out behind a counter with a protecting grille above it. Away to the left was the shop part of the establishment where there were shelves of confectionery and provisions. On the right was a heavy iron safe standing under the counter.

"Ah!" Duggan said, as the torchlight fell on the safe. "There she is. There's the little beauty."

To Fawley it looked anything but a beauty. It was old and had obviously had a lot of use. For a professional safe-breaker it would probably be a simple job to open it; but was Duggan a professional? It seemed unlikely. And what about the people who were almost certainly asleep in the house? Any work of safe-cracking would surely waken them even though the breaking-in had not.

"So what now?" he asked.

"Now," Duggan said, "we open the safe. What else are we here for?"

"With the jemmy?"

"Talk sense," Duggan said.

"How, then?"

"We get the man to do it for us."

"What man?"

"The sub-postmaster, of course. Who did you think I meant?"

He was asleep in one of the bedrooms, lying in a double bed with his wife beside him. There was no one else in the house; Duggan had checked on that; there were two other bedrooms but they were unoccupied.

The sub-postmaster was a grossly fat man and he was wearing blue-and-white striped pyjamas. His hair was thinning and there was a dark shadow of stubble on his cheeks and chin. His wife was almost as fat as he was; she had a hairnet on her head and her face had an oddly crumpled appearance like a punctured balloon.

They had both been sleeping soundly and neither had wakened until Duggan had switched on the bedside lamp and pushed the muzzle of a revolver into the folds of flesh under the man's chin.

"Don't do anything stupid," Duggan said. "Just do as you're told and maybe you'll live to tell your grandchildren about it."

Fawley made a mental note of the fact that he had been right in thinking Duggan would be armed. The revolver had a short barrel which would have made it easy to carry in the pocket.

The woman let out a squawk when she saw the revolver and what Duggan was doing with it. The man was making no sound at all; he appeared to be petrified with fright. But the woman was making enough noise for both of them and to Fawley it seemed that the sound of her screeching would rouse the whole village.

Duggan turned his head and snarled at her savagely: "Stop that!"

She went on screeching as if she had not heard him.

"For Christ's sake!" Duggan said. "Why don't somebody do something about that bitch? She'll bring the bloody fire brigade."

Fawley had a feeling that he was the one who was expected to do something. But what? Gag her with a pillow? Give her a clout on the head with his pistol? He had still done nothing when Molly stepped up to the bed and slapped the woman hard on the mouth with the flat of her hand.

It put a stop to the screeching. The woman's face seemed to crumple a bit more and a trickle of blood came from her upper lip. She began to weep silently, the tears running down her cheeks and losing themselves in the folds of skin. She had the look of a whipped child.

Duggan spoke again to the man. "Now you're going to come with us and open the safe."

"No," the man said. He sounded hoarse.

Duggan pushed the revolver muzzle deeper into the flesh of his chin. "Now don't be awkward. We can do some nasty things to you. We can do nastier things to your old woman. And in the end you'll have to do it."

"Do it, George," the woman said, her voice trembling. "They'll kill us else. Do what the man says. Please."

"Now there's somebody with a bit of sense," Duggan said. "You hear that, George? So how about it? Are you going to do it the easy way or the hard way? It's your choice."

The sub-postmaster made no further resistance. The initial refusal had been no more than a token, a small tribute to his official duty. But he was not a fool and he could see that there was no point in trying to play the hero; it would only result in much physical pain for himself and his wife, and in the end he would be forced to co-operate.

"All right," he said. "Take the gun away and let me get up."

There was a rather grubby dressing-gown hanging on a hook on the door, and when he had rolled out of the bed he pulled this over his pyjamas and shoved his feet into a pair of carpet slippers.

Molly pointed at the woman, who was still lying in the bed. "What about her?"

"We'll leave you to deal with her," Duggan said. "Tie her up. You'd better gag her too, in case she starts squawking again. You can manage that?"

"I can manage it," Molly said. "She won't give any trouble. Will you, missis?"

The woman shook her head dumbly. It was quite apparent that she was far too scared to offer any resistance to the binding and gagging.

"Let's go, then," Duggan said. "Time's money."

There was about five thousand pounds in cash in the safe. There were stamps and postal-orders also, but Duggan was not interested in them. He put the money in the hold-all and took out the jemmy. He grinned at the fat man with a sudden ugly baring of the teeth. It was not a pleasant grin and the man looked nervous.

"You've been very helpful," Duggan said. "Without your co-operation it might have been a real hard job to open that safe. So to show just how grateful we are I'm going to give you a reward."

The man backed away a step or two until he was brought to a halt by the counter. He stared fearfully at the iron bar in Duggan's hand. "I don't want any reward. You've got what you came for. Why don't you just go?"

'Oh, we'll go, never you fear. But first the reward. You must have it; I won't take a refusal."

Duggan raised the jemmy in his right hand, took a quick step forward and hit the man on the side of the face. There was a sharp cracking sound which might have been a bone breaking. The man uttered a cry of pain and fell to the floor, a grotesque groaning mound of flesh in the blue dressing-gown. Duggan moved in and hit him again, raining blows on the unprotected head.

Fawley was appalled by the ferocity of the unprovoked attack. He grabbed Duggan's arm.

"Lay off it! You'll kill him. What are you doing?"

Duggan stopped hitting the man. There was blood on the victim's head, blood on the dressing-gown, blood on the floor and on the jemmy.

"What's up, Clyde? Can't you take a bit of violence? Is your stomach too weak?"

"But there was no need. He hadn't made any trouble. So why this?"

The man on the floor was not groaning now; he was making no sound and no movement.

"He's a Brit," Duggan said. "He's the enemy. And besides, we wouldn't want him getting on the blower to the coppers as soon as we walked away."

"We could have tied him up."

"Why trouble? This way was easier."

Duggan wiped the jemmy on the sub-postmaster's dressing-gown, put it back in the hold-all and fastened the zipper.

"You've killed him," Fawley said.

Duggan shook his head. "I doubt it. He'll live. And he'll be able to say he put up a fight. This could make him a hero."

Molly came into the room. "You finished here?"

"Just packing up and ready to go," Duggan said.

She looked at the unconscious man with no apparent sense of shock. "Did he give you trouble?"

"None to speak of. You managed all right upstairs?"

"Oh, fine. The old girl didn't lift a finger. She was scared out of her mind."

"Let's be on our way, then."

Fawley pointed at the sub-postmaster. "You're going to leave him like that?"

"How else would you expect me to leave him?" Duggan asked.

"He needs medical aid."

"So what if he does? It's not our worry."

"What's the matter with our Clyde?" Molly asked.

"I don't think he approves of the rough stuff."

The girl looked at Fawley with mockery in her eyes. "Is that so, Clyde? Are you afraid of a little blood?"

"No," Fawley said. "But I just don't see that it was necessary."

He was sickened by the gratuitous violence, the sadistic manner of Duggan's attack on the fat man; sickened too by the callousness of the girl, who apparently saw nothing in it to deplore. Was this the effect that being engaged in this struggle had on the participants? Did it harden them, blunt their feelings, until they had no regard for any suffering they might cause to innocent people? And would he eventually become no less callous than they?

Duggan picked up the hold-all. "Let's go."

Fawley went with the other two. He had taken part in a sordid criminal act and he felt soiled and ashamed. For despite Duggan's assurance that it had been a necessary operation, there was no way in which he could reconcile this mean and dirty robbery with his once-bright vision of fighting for the cause of a united Ireland.

Connolly was waiting for them in the car. "You took your time." He sounded peevish.

Duggan just threw the hold-all in and got in beside him, leaving Fawley and Molly to sit in the back. Connolly had the car moving even before the doors were shut. There was still no sign that anyone was awake in the village.

The Cortina was where they had left it. They changed cars quickly and abandoned the stolen Vauxhall which had served its purpose. Soon they were back in the sprawling mass of Greater London.

Raven House was silent and apparently lifeless when Fawley climbed the stairs to his room. He had got out of the Cortina a few streets away and had walked the last part of the homeward journey, meeting no one. In his room he kicked off his shoes and lay on the bed without bothering to undress. He was unable to sleep; in his mind he kept going over again and again the events of the night and finding in them nothing to give him a shred of comfort.

He thought once more of the possibility of walking out on the other three, ignoring the threat to his safety if he did so. But he could not make up his mind to take the step, even though he had been thoroughly sickened by what had occurred. He wondered what his uncle, Daniel O'Higgins, would have done in such a situation. Would he have had any qualms regarding the post office robbery or would he have accepted it without question as something that was necessary to the cause and therefore essential and perhaps even laudable?

Fawley, having thought about it, was forced to the conclusion that O'Higgins probably would. Unhappily, this conclusion did nothing to dispel his own misgivings.

He slept at last, but his dreams were troubled, and when he awoke in the morning he felt depressed and unrefreshed.

Chapter Eight – GOOD SAMARITAN

Fawley encountered Rita Woolley on the stairs as he was about to leave the house. She seemed to be in a bright and cheerful mood, which contrasted sharply with his own feeling of acute depression. His lack of spirits must have been apparent, for she took one look at him and said with some concern:

"Is anything wrong, Clyde? You don't look at all well. I hope you're not ill."

"No," Fawley said. "I'm okay. I slept badly, that's all. I'm not feeling as chipper as I might."

"Something on your mind?"

He glanced at her keenly. "No. Why should there be?"

"Oh, I don't know. I just thought you might be worried about something and it kept you awake."

"There's nothing for me to be worried about, nothing at all."

"Well, that's good to know. Most of us have loads to worry us. Me, I worry about money. Don't you?"

"Frankly, no," Fawley said. "Money is no problem for me."

"No? Lucky old you. But you're looking pretty down in the mouth all the same. Maybe you're working too hard."

"Working too hard!"

"At the book."

"Oh, that! Yes, maybe I am."

"I'd say what you need is a bit more relaxation. Have you got any friends in London?"

"No, but –"

"There you are, then. You're too much on your own. You need someone to take you out of yourself." Miss Woolley treated him to a winning smile and he had to admit to himself that she really was an attractive girl, even if at the moment she was making herself something of a nuisance.

"Look," she said, "I have a lot of time on my hands just now and I'd be only too happy to guide you round the pleasure spots, if you see what I mean. What do you say? Does it appeal to you?"

Fawley had a feeling of embarrassment. He wanted to get away from Miss Woolley, but the position in which she had planted herself on the narrow staircase prevented him from getting past without pushing her aside, which would have been an act of rudeness that was not in his nature to commit. And the curious fact was that he had a ridiculous urge to confide in her, to share with her all his worries and problems concerning the IRA cell with which he had become involved and the uncertainty regarding what he ought to do. There was something so warm and friendly, so comforting even, about this lovely blonde girl that she seemed to invite confidence merely by being there.

But it would have been madness, of course. What he had to tell would have sent her running to the police, and then there would have been the devil to pay. He had to keep it to himself, work things out in his own way without help from any other person.

"I'm sorry," he said. "I don't really think it's on. Thanks all the same."

"Well, it's up to you, of course. But if you ask me, I think we could have fun. After all, I'm not exactly repulsive, am I?"

Miss Woolley was wearing stretch-cord jeans which fitted snugly round her buttocks and accentuated their smooth curves, with a pale-blue knitted jumper which did as much for the upper half of her body. Her nose was retroussé, her eyes large and her hair was a honey-gold in colour. Anyone less repulsive to the male of the species it would have been difficult to imagine.

"No," Fawley said. "You're very attractive."

She seemed delighted to hear it. "Do you think so – really? You're not just saying that to make me feel good?"

"No; I mean it."

"Well, then –"

"It's not possible. Not just now. I have things to do." He began to edge his way past her.

"Well, think about it. You take things too seriously. You should have some joy in your life. Everyone should have joy in their lives."

Fawley thought she could be right at that; but he could see little prospect of any joy in his life at the present time. He left the house and abandoned Miss Woolley to her own devices, whatever they might have been.

He bought a couple of morning papers at the newsagent's down the road and went to a small teashop nearby for a cup of coffee. Sitting at a table by himself he opened one of the newspapers and hunted for a report of the post office robbery. He went through the pages from the front to the back and found no mention of it. He searched the other paper with the same result. He wondered whether such an incident was not important enough to warrant a Press report; but then it occurred to him that a more likely reason for its non-appearance was that news of the robbery had come in too late to catch the early papers.

He had no radio, and he had an impulse to call on Duggan and the others to inquire whether they had heard anything. But he dismissed this idea because he guessed that he would not have been very welcome at the builder's yard. He had been warned to stay away from there unless Duggan got in touch with him, and it would be wise to heed the warning.

To pass the time he travelled up to the West End and wandered aimlessly around, looking into shop windows and studying the posters outside the theatres. He browsed among the bookshops in Charing Cross Road, and as soon as the evening papers hit the streets he bought one and glanced through it avidly.

The report was there, with a photograph of the post office and police cars parked on the forecourt. It appeared that a postman arriving for work had discovered the break-in and had called the police. Mr Seppings, the sub-postmaster, was lying near the open safe covered in blood and with severe injuries to the head. It was evident that he had been savagely attacked with a bludgeon of some description. He was now in intensive care in hospital, but he was in a coma and his condition was critical.

Mrs Seppings had been discovered lying on her bed, bound hand and foot and gagged with strips of torn-up sheet. She was still in a state of shock and had been unable to give any very clear description of the robbers; all she could say for certain was that there had been three of them, two men and a young woman, that they had all been wearing balaclava helmets and carrying guns, and that one of the men and the woman had spoken with Scottish accents. The other man had said nothing.

"Scottish accents?" Fawley murmured. It was an odd mistake to make, but perhaps a fortunate one.

There was no mention of the get-away car. Perhaps it had not yet been discovered. But even if it had there would be nothing about it to suggest that it might have been connected with the robbery at the post office. And they had taken care to leave no fingerprints.

Fawley got rid of the paper and felt a trifle easier in his mind. It was a relief to learn that the sub-postmaster was not dead, though he might yet die, and then it would become a murder investigation. Fawley prayed that he would survive, but it would be no thanks to Duggan if he did.

The report mentioned a sum of about four or five thousand pounds having been stolen. It was a contemptibly small amount when all was said and done; certainly not enough to warrant such violence and possibly murder. He himself could have got the money simply by putting a call through to his uncle. O'Higgins would have dipped into his pocket without a moment's hesitation; and he would not have had to dip very deeply, either.

But it would not have been according to the book, and though he had a feeling that Duggan might have made no objection, he had to play it by the book even if the contents of that volume were proving less and less to his taste.

It was early evening when he returned to Raven House, and he had not been in his room for more than a few seconds when there was a tap on the door. When he opened it he discovered Rita Woolley standing there. She must, he thought, have been keeping watch for his return.

"Oh," she said, "so you are back. May I come in?"

Once again she walked in without waiting for his permission and he was left with one hand on the door, wondering whether he ought to close it or leave it open in the hope that Miss Woolley's business with him would not take long and that she would soon leave. Seeing, however, that she had sat herself down in one of the armchairs and was giving no indication of any intention of making an early departure he came to the conclusion that for the sake of privacy it might be best to close the door, and this he did.

"Was there something you wanted to see me about?" he asked, regarding her with some uneasiness.

"Yes," she said. "I've been thinking things over and I've decided to be a good Samaritan."

Fawley looked puzzled. "I don't quite understand. You'd better explain that."

"It's quite simple. I'm going to take you in hand."

"But that's nonsense. What makes you imagine I need any taking in hand? Whatever that may mean."

"Well, it's obvious, isn't it? Here you are in a strange country, all by yourself, with no friend, no one to talk to, no one to confide in. It's no wonder you're feeling depressed."

"Who said I was depressed?"

"Nobody has to say it; it's plain to see. You're not going to deny it, are you?"

"What if I did?"

"I wouldn't believe you."

"Well," Fawley said, "even if I am feeling a bit dispirited right now, there's nothing you can do about it."

"Wrong," she said. "There's a great deal I can do about it, and I intend to."

"But even if you could, which seems most unlikely, why should you?'

She smiled at him. "Maybe because I've taken a liking to you, Clyde. I think deep down you're really rather a nice sort of person, aren't you?"

Fawley made no answer.

"So that's why I'm not going to take no for an answer. I shall just sit here in this chair until you agree to it even if I have to stay here all night."

"Agree to what, for Pete's sake?"

"To come out with me. We'll go places. I'll show you round. You'll enjoy it; I promise."

"You don't have to bother. I can take care of myself."

"I'm not so sure about that. Anyway, it wouldn't be any bother. I shall enjoy it too."

Fawley gave a fleeting grin. In spite of himself he could not help being amused by Miss Woolley's insistence on playing the good Samaritan on his behalf. "So it's not altogether altruistic?"

"Altru what?"

"Istic. What I mean is you're not making this offer entirely for my benefit. You stand to get something out of it yourself."

"Maybe. But that's no reason why you shouldn't accept the offer. It'll be a sort of give and take. What do you say?"

He shook his head. "I'm afraid it's still not on."

She sighed heavily, making quite a meal of it. "Then I shall just have to sit here until it is on."

He regarded her with a wry, thoughtful expression. She had settled herself very firmly in the armchair and seemed to have every intention of doing what she had threatened.

"I really believe you would."

"You can count on it."

"I think you'd get rather tired of sitting there and doing nothing."

"And you might get tired of having me here. It'd be a question of which of us was the first to weaken. But there's no sense in letting it come to that, is there? I mean, what have you got to lose by falling in with my suggestion? It won't kill you."

Fawley thought about it. What indeed did he have to lose? And maybe she was right; perhaps he did need some distraction. It would at least be better than sitting alone in his room and brooding on the events of the previous night.

"Okay," he said. "You win."

"So you'll come?"

"You don't give me much choice, do you?"

She made no attempt to conceal her delight. "I'm so glad; I really am. And we'll both be winners; you'll see." She got up from the chair. "How soon can you be ready?"

"Give me ten minutes."

She was back promptly when the ten minutes were up. She was carrying a shoulder-bag and had made a pretty quick change from the jeans to a blue denim skirt and jacket.

"All set?" she asked.

"All set," Fawley said.

"Should we go, then?"

He had had some doubts about the wisdom of it when he had allowed her to talk him into accepting the invitation to which she had refused to take no for an answer, but in the event he was glad she had been so insistent. As things turned out it was an evening to remember. Indeed, he had not had such a thoroughly enjoyable experience since relations with the faithless Jackie Dring had been so abruptly and unfortunately terminated. He had almost forgotten what he had been missing.

Not that there was anything particularly remarkable about the programme of entertainment laid on by Miss Woolley: a meal in a crowded coffee bar frequented almost exclusively by exuberant and talkative young people, followed by a visit to an even more crowded discotheque where his eyes were dazzled by the glittering coloured lights and his ears assaulted by the sheer volume of sound that filled the place could hardly have been described as a once-in-a-lifetime evening on the town. It was simply the presence of Miss Woolley herself that made it for him. For the plain fact of the matter was that the longer he spent in the company of this good

Samaritan the more he warmed to her and the more he wanted to be with her.

"You are enjoying it, aren't you?" she said.

Fawley had to admit that he was.

"I knew you would. You should do this more often."

"Maybe I will," he said.

He knew that it was not the purpose for which he had come to London, but somehow that purpose no longer had so great an attraction for him; there were other things in life and perhaps they were more important after all.

He was paying for everything. Miss Woolley was perfectly willing to allow him to do so, for he had assured her that he was not short of money, and she unfortunately was; indeed with her it seemed to be an almost permanent condition.

It was late when they returned to Raven House. Miss Woolley suggested a cup of coffee in her room and Fawley made no objection. The room was basically similar to his own, but it had the imprint of its occupant. It was untidy, cluttered, dusty, but there was a friendly welcoming quality about it which was lacking in that other room across the landing. When they had drunk the coffee he felt no inclination to leave and Miss Woolley was not urging him to go.

He stood up. "Well," he said, "it's been great; it surely has. I can't remember when I had a more enjoyable evening."

He was half-turned towards the door but was making no move towards it. Rita Woolley advanced towards him and put her arms round his neck. He kissed her, holding her a little stiffly but feeling a sudden quickening of the pulse.

"You know," he said, "I think I'm beginning to fall in love with you."

She laughed. "Now you're being silly, Clyde."

He was hurt by her reaction, though he understood that she was merely being realistic. But he meant what he had said. It was the truth.

"Would it really be so silly?"

She did not laugh this time. "I do believe you're serious."

"Why wouldn't I be serious? Is it so unbelievable?"

"I don't know. It's just – well, it just doesn't happen like this, does it?"

"What do you mean, it doesn't happen like this? How does it happen, for God's sake?"

She made no answer to that. She said: "You don't know anything about me."

"What in hell has that to do with it?" Fawley demanded.

She disengaged herself from him and moved away. "You're a funny boy, you know."

"I'm not a boy; I'm a man."

"Yes, of course. But you're very young."

"Not so young at that. Anyway, let's forget about age. Are you saying you don't love me?"

"Why, Clyde," she said, "it never occurred to me. I haven't thought about it."

"Think about it now."

She gave him a long intent look. Then she said: "I like you, of course. I think I like you more than any man I ever knew. Maybe I could even fall in love with you. But give it time. Don't rush me."

Fawley shrugged. "Okay, let's give it time. Do you want me to go now?"

"Do you want to go?"

"No," Fawley said.

She smiled at him. "Then you'd better stay, hadn't you? Like I said before, everyone should have some joy in their lives."

Chapter Nine – NICE GIRL

They had breakfast together. It was a scratch meal made up of odds and ends culled from Miss Woolley's larder. Fawley had told Molly he did not eat breakfast, but he made an exception in this case. It was the company that did it.

"What have you got planned for today?" she asked.

"Nothing," Fawley said.

"Nor me. So how about seeing a few of the sights of London?"

"With you as guide?"

"Of course."

"That sounds like a good idea," Fawley said.

He was not sure whether Duggan would want to get in touch with him, but he saw no reason why he should hang around in his room waiting to be summoned to the builder's yard. Let Duggan wait.

For the first part of the day things could hardly have been better. The weather was warm for early spring and the sunlight lent an added enchantment to the scene. Miss Woolley was not the most methodical of guides, but Fawley was not bothered by the haphazard nature of the sightseeing; for him it was enough simply to be in her company. He had only a hazy idea of where she was taking him, but he caught a glimpse of the Houses of Parliament and Westminster Abbey, the Horse Guards and Buckingham Palace and a variety of other places of interest. At some time in the late afternoon they found themselves in Piccadilly Circus and it was as they were strolling up Regent Street that the day became suddenly marred.

It was only later, reading about it in the papers, that they were to learn the full details of the atrocity, to realize that the bomb had been planted in one of the large shops and apparently detonated by remote control, killing twenty-five people and injuring many others. At the time they were aware only of a tremendous explosion, of flying glass and falling masonry, of bodies lying in the street, of people screaming, of blood, of severed limbs, of a smell of burning.

They were close enough to feel the blast, far enough away to escape injury to themselves. Rita gave a cry and clutched at Fawley's arm.

"Oh, God! Oh, my God!"

He was stunned, unable for the moment to move, even to think clearly. Then his brain began to work normally and he knew what he had to do.

"I must help."

"No, Clyde. There's nothing you can do. Let's get away from here."

But already he was moving towards the devastated building, breaking into a run. She ran beside him, tugging at his sleeve, trying to stop him.

"No, Clyde, no! You can't do any good."

It was a scene of utter confusion. People were wandering around in a daze, traffic had come to a halt, a car was lying on its side, there was glass everywhere. There was a small child covered in blood, its face no longer recognizable. A woman, possibly its mother, was kneeling beside it, distraught, fondling this small mutilated object and moaning softly. A man was sitting on the kerb and cursing; his left sleeve was in tatters and blood was dripping from the arm.

The police were beginning to arrive; an ambulance drove up, then others; a fire-engine appeared. The men in uniform were quickly taking charge with professional efficiency; some began to treat the injured while others erected barriers and started to clear the disaster area of those who were simply standing idly around and gazing with a kind of ghoulish fascination at the victims of the bombing. Fawley saw that Miss Woolley had been right; there was nothing useful he could do and like the gawkers he was merely in the way.

He turned to his companion. "Okay, let's go."

She was only too willing to do so. They walked away in the direction of Oxford Circus and did not look back. Rita muttered something which he did not catch.

"What did you say?"

She answered with a vehemence that surprised him. "I said bloody IRA swine."

"You think they were the people who did it?"

"Who else would it have been?"

"I don't know. There are other groups who plant bombs, aren't there?"

"Maybe there are, but I bet the IRA did this. It's the sort of thing they've done before, killing innocent people. They're bloody murderers, that's what they are; the whole gang of them ought to be shot; though shooting's too good for them." She turned on Fawley with sudden accusation. "And these are the criminals people in your country raise funds to support. Do you know that? They collect money for them so that they can buy weapons and explosives. Bastards!"

Fawley was not sure whether the last word was intended to refer to the IRA or their American supporters. Perhaps both. He was silent. What could he say? How could he defend people who resorted to the kind of barbarism he had just witnessed? Could any cause, however worthy, justify such methods?

He felt confused in his mind, not knowing what to say. One thing was certain: if Rita Woolley had had the least suspicion that he was one of those Americans who supported the IRA she would have turned away from him in utter revulsion and disgust. She would have been horrified; to her it would have been as though she had been consorting with a monster. This was all too apparent to him now, and the realization was like the stab of a knife.

"Let's go home," she said.

There was nothing else to do. The Regent Street bomb had ruined the day for them and they could take no more pleasure in sightseeing. With mutual agreement they left the late afternoon sunshine and went down into the artificial light of Oxford Circus Underground Station.

*

Making love to Rita Woolley, Fawley could not avoid a sense of shame and guilt. He felt that he was deceiving her, and he again had a crazy impulse to tell her everything; the reason for his presence in London, his connection with the IRA cell, even the story of the post office robbery. But he knew that there was no way he could have justified his actions to her; it would have been of no use telling her of that dream he had had since boyhood, the dream of fighting for a golden cause, the cause of a free and united Ireland. She would never have understood.

And the truth was that he could no longer view it in the same light that once had made it a brilliant and glittering jewel; now it had become dulled and he doubted whether for him it could ever be made to shine brightly again. All that was finished.

In the morning he received a message from Duggan; it was a summons to the builder's yard. He went with gloom in his heart.

"Where were you yesterday?" Duggan demanded. "We tried to contact you."

"I was out."

"All day?"

"Yes, all day."

"What were you doing?"

"Looking at London."

"You mean sightseeing?" Duggan sounded incredulous, as though this were something it was almost impossible to believe.

"You could call it that."

"Well, for the love of Mike!" Connolly said. "Sightseeing! With us looking for him all over."

"Maybe he thinks he's here for a holiday," Molly said. "Like he came on a package tour."

They were all there, all three of them, in the house adjoining the builder's yard. There seemed to be very little doing in the repairing and decorating line.

"I didn't know I was so essential to you," Fawley said. "You've never given me that impression."

"Maybe not," Duggan said. "But you should be around when we want to contact you."

"Well, I'm here now. So what's it all about?"

"There was an incident in London yesterday. Regent Street. Did you hear about it?"

"I didn't need to hear about it. I was there."

They stared at him.

"You were there?" Molly said. "You mean on the spot when the bomb went off?"

"Near enough to feel the blast."

"Well, think of that now!" Duggan said. "There's a coincidence."

"Do you know who planted it?" Fawley asked.

"Some of our lads."

"Did you know about it? Beforehand, I mean."

"No, of course not. Do you think we all get told? Do you think they pass the information round like a theatre programme? I don't even know the ones that carried out the operation. I don't want to know. It's best this way. The coppers were here last night, you know."

Fawley was startled. "The police! About the post office job?"

"No. You can forget that. It was routine. Whenever there's a bombing in London they come asking questions. Where were we at the time? Do we know anything? They nose around, hunting for weapons or explosives. They never find anything. Not here."

"Why do they pick on you?."

"Because we're Irish. And Catholic. That makes us suspect in their book."

"I see," Fawley said. "Is this what you wanted to talk to me about?"

"No. We were looking for you before the bombing happened. Something else came up." Duggan turned to the girl. "Where's the paper, Moll?"

"I'll get it," she said. She went out of the room and came back a minute later with a newspaper in her hand. "Here you are."

Duggan took the paper from her and folded it so that an item of news was uppermost. He handed the folded paper to Fawley, stabbing the report with his forefinger.

"Have you seen this? It's yesterday's paper."

"I didn't see a newspaper yesterday," Fawley said. There had been other things to occupy his time.

"Well, read it. You should find it interesting."

Fawley looked at the headline and knew why Duggan had said he would be interested. It read: "IRA GUN-RUNNERS CAUGHT".

He glanced rapidly through the report and learned that a fishing-boat had been intercepted off the west coast of Ireland by a patrol vessel of the Irish Navy. The fishing-boat had attempted to escape and shots had been fired, forcing it to heave to. A boarding party had been transferred from the naval vessel and a search had revealed a quantity of arms and ammunition and explosives in the hold of the fishing-boat. These supplies had been destined for the Provisional IRA and were to have been smuggled ashore. It was believed that the cargo had been brought from the United States in a larger vessel and had been transhipped at a rendezvous outside Irish territorial waters.

There was a good deal more to the report, but Fawley had got the gist of it in the first few lines. There was no mention of the name of the larger vessel, the ship that had brought the cargo from America, but he had no need to be told that it was that same small ageing freighter with the rust stains on its hull which he had boarded in New York in company with his uncle and a skinny little Irishman named Michael Grady. He was surprised that Captain Brown's ship should have taken so long to cross the Atlantic; but when he came to think about it maybe it had not been so long at that; it merely seemed so to him because so much had happened in the few short weeks since his arrival in Dublin.

The others had been watching him closely while he was reading, and when he looked up from the paper he met their eyes and detected in them a hint of suspicion, even of accusation perhaps.

"What do you think of it?" Duggan asked.

"I think it's unfortunate."

"Unfortunate, is it? Oh, to be sure, most unfortunate. And I wonder why. Why would that naval boat be there just at that particular time, do you think?"

"I don't know."

"And I don't know, either. Maybe I have ideas, though. Tell me, Clyde, did you know anything about that shipment? Before you came over here, I mean."

"Well, yes," Fawley admitted, "I guess I did." It had to be the same one; there would not have been two shipments so close together. "In fact I was on board the ship that brought the stuff from the States just before I left New York. My uncle –" He stopped abruptly. It had occurred to him that perhaps he was talking too much, revealing matters that would have been better kept to himself.

"Go on," Duggan said. "What were you going to say about your uncle?"

"Nothing."

"Oh, sure you were. Your uncle's a big wheel in all this, isn't he? You don't have to be shy about admitting it; you're among friends here, you know. Maybe he was the one who arranged the shipment. Am I right?"

"He was involved, yes."

"Sure he was. And that's how you came to know all about it, isn't it?"

"Yes. But I don't see what this has to do with –"

"Somebody blew it," Connolly said.

"Oh, look now," Fawley said. "You don't think I –"

"We don't know what to think," Duggan said. "All we know is that somebody must have played the informer and you had the opportunity. You can't deny that."

"But this is crazy. Why would I do such a thing? I came over here because I wanted to help you, didn't I?"

"So you say."

"Don't you believe me?"

"Why should we believe you?" Molly demanded.

Fawley lifted his hands, palms upward, in a gesture of helplessness. How could he convince them he was telling the truth? There was no way he could prove he was not an informer. Who could have imagined it would come to this? That his high-minded offer of himself to the cause would bring suspicions of treachery on his head.

"For God's sake!" he said. "What possible motive could I have had for such a betrayal? Ever since I was a kid I've supported the Republican cause."

He had a feeling that he was getting through to them. They looked at one another, and then Duggan said:

"All right; you've got a point there. So maybe we'll give you the benefit of the doubt. But you'd better take care not to step out of line."

"I've no intention of stepping out of line."

"Good. Then we'll take your word for it. This time."

Fawley left soon after that. Duggan came with him into the yard and gave him a word of instruction before he departed.

"Keep yourself in readiness, Clyde. There's something coming up and we may need you."

"What is it?" Fawley asked.

"Never mind what it is, but just be ready. All right?"

"All right," Fawley said.

But he was not sure it was all right. He was not sure he wanted to have anything to do with it – whatever it was.

*

About an hour after Fawley had gone another visitor turned up at the builder's yard. He was a thin, sad-looking man wearing a dark grey suit, a black trench-coat, black shoes and a bowler hat. He arrived on foot, having paid off his taxi some distance away, and he was carrying a briefcase in one hand. He looked like a salesman, but he was not selling anything and what he talked about was certainly not building material.

Duggan treated him with considerable deference and addressed him as Mr Finnegan, bringing out a bottle of Irish whiskey in his honour. Mr Finnegan accepted the offer of stimulant, and then the three men and the girl went into a huddle and had a long discussion which ended when the visitor got up and announced that it was time for him to go.

"So now," he said, "you know what you have to do."

"Now we know," Duggan said. "You can depend on us, Mr Finnegan."

"I hope so," Finnegan said; and he looked hard at Duggan with his sharp little eyes that were oddly like those of a small vicious rodent. "I surely hope I can."

*

Fawley was surprised by his own reaction to the news of the interception of the arms shipment. The reaction had been immediate and spontaneous. He was glad.

It was amazing that in such a brief space of time his entire attitude to the IRA should have undergone so complete a change. It was not that he no longer believed in the desirability of a united Ireland; he did. But he could not approve or even condone the methods employed by the Provos to achieve that objective. Nothing could justify the slaughter of innocent people. It was a wonder to him that he should not have appreciated this before; but things had appeared so different from a distance of thousands of miles. Now that he had seen for himself at close quarters what the bombing campaign really entailed his eyes had been opened to the callous brutality of it all. He remembered the child covered in blood, the distraught mother, the dead and the maimed; he remembered too the sadistic viciousness of Duggan's attack on the sub-postmaster and felt sickened to think that he should have had any part in it.

And yet Uncle Danny would probably greet the news of the Regent Street bombing with satisfaction and would drink a toast with his cronies to the brave lads who had perpetrated the atrocity. They would not be so happy about the loss of the arms shipment; that would be a big disappointment to them. And again he felt glad.

It was curious, Fawley reflected, that Duggan and the other two should have suspected him of giving information to the police about the smuggling operation. It had never so much as entered his head to do so; yet now if the opportunity had occurred again he might have felt inclined to do just that. Such was the measure of his change of heart.

On his return to Raven House he encountered Miss Wills in the narrow entrance hall. Her pleasure in seeing him was evident in the way her small wrinkled face seemed to light up.

"Why, Mr Fawley! How nice to see you again. I did so enjoy our little chat the other day."

"I enjoyed it, too," Fawley said. And it was not altogether untrue.

"Did you? Did you really? You're not just saying that to please an old woman?"

"Certainly not."

"Well, you must come again. I've got some more photographs to show you. How about this evening?"

"I'm sorry," Fawley said. "This evening I already have an engagement."

Miss Wills looked arch. "It wouldn't, I suppose, be with a young lady who lives not a hundred miles from here?"

Fawley smiled but said nothing. It was evident that Miss Wills kept her eyes and ears open and was quick to put two and two together. She gave his hand a friendly pat and spoke confidentially.

"I'm so glad. Miss Woolley is a very nice girl. So helpful. And things haven't always been easy for her, poor dear. You like her, don't you?"

"Yes, I like her."

"And of course she thinks the world of you."

Fawley was startled. "Did she tell you that?"

"Not in so many words. But I can tell, I can read between the lines. And I wish you both every happiness."

It seemed to Fawley that Miss Wills was leaping ahead and already hearing wedding bells and all that sort of thing. She probably had a romantic nature and perhaps her ideas of life were still influenced by all those musical comedies she had danced her way through so many years ago.

"Well," she said, "I mustn't keep you, Mr Fawley. I'm sure you have lots to do. I'm just going to do a little shopping." She was carrying a small basket on her arm with a worn leather purse inside it. It looked horribly easy to snatch. "I trust you're enjoying your stay in this country."

"Oh, yes," Fawley said.

It was only half the truth, but he could not tell her the whole of it.

"That's good," Miss Wills said. "Take my advice; make the most of things while you're young. Life's not nearly as much fun when you're old."

"I'll try to remember that," Fawley said.

Chapter Ten – *SOMETHING WRONG*

Fawley had another summons from Duggan the next morning. He went to the builder's yard and found Duggan and Molly in the house. Connolly appeared not to be there and the pick-up truck was nowhere to be seen, so it looked as though he might have gone off somewhere to carry out a legitimate job in the building and decorating line.

Molly was in the kitchen doing something with vegetables at the sink. There was a cigarette in her mouth and the smoke was getting in her eyes. Fawley had given a rap on the door and walked in without ceremony.

"So it's you, is it?" she said. She sounded neither friendly nor unfriendly; just neutral.

"It's me," Fawley said. "I had an order to come here."

"Pat's in the office. You'd better go through. He's expecting you."

"He would be, wouldn't he?"

Duggan was seated at the desk when Fawley walked in. There was a black attaché-case lying on the desk with a key in the lock.

"So you got the message this time," Duggan said.

"Yes, I got it. What's it all about?"

"A job," Duggan said. "For you. Solus."

"What kind of job?"

"Delivery." Duggan tapped the attaché-case with his finger. "This."

Fawley stared at the case in puzzlement. "You're asking me to deliver that?" It seemed a petty sort of job to come all the way from America to do. An errand boy could have done as much.

'Not asking you," Duggan said. "Ordering you. Maybe you didn't realize it, but when you joined us you became a soldier. No uniform, no badge, but a soldier just the same. I'm your superior officer and when I give an order you jump to it. Understand?"

"If you say so."

"I do say so."

"What am I delivering in the case? Something important, is it?"

"It's important sure enough. Take a look."

Duggan opened the attaché-case and Fawley took a look. Inside was a contraption of wires and batteries and various other components. There was also a kind of clock or timer, together with a small slab of grey substance rather like putty. Fawley had never seen anything like it before, but he had no doubt that what he was looking at was a time-bomb and it gave him an odd sort of feeling, as if the hairs on his scalp had stiffened suddenly.

"You know what this is?" Duggan asked.

"I can guess," Fawley said. He should have known that it would not be just a matter of taking an innocent piece of luggage from one place to another, not a job that an errand boy could have done. He should have realized immediately Duggan tapped the attaché-case with his finger that there was more to it than that. "It's a bomb, isn't it?"

"Right in one, sonny boy."

"And where are you asking – ordering me to deliver it?"

"Paddington Station."

Fawley said nothing. He was thinking. And what he was thinking was that he did not like the sound of it. He had seen what mayhem a bomb could cause and now he was being asked – no, ordered – to plant just such a device himself. This one might be a lot smaller than the Regent Street bomb, but it was capable of causing a lot of damage and even death, nevertheless.

He thought of telling Duggan outright that he would not do it, but he realized that he was in a tricky situation and would be well advised to act with caution. These were dangerous people he was dealing with; people who might react with violence if he refused to play the game their way. He had let himself become involved with them and now it might be difficult and even risky to pull back.

"Now this is the way you'll do it," Duggan said. "You'll take the case to your room and keep it there until tomorrow. Tomorrow morning you'll set the timing – I'll show you how to do that – and you'll go by tube train to Paddington Station. Ever been there before?"

"No."

"It's easy enough. Second station from Notting Hill Gate. You should get there in not more than half an hour from your bed-sit."

"Why do I have to keep the bomb in my room? Why can't I pick it up here tomorrow?"

"Because it'll be safer this way. The coppers might come here again sniffing round."

"Where do I plant the bomb at Paddington?"

"In one of the left-luggage lockers. You'll set the timer before you leave Raven House. Give it a couple of hours to be on the safe side."

"How do I do that?"

"It's simple. You just turn this knob here until the correct figure comes up on the dial. Then you put that switch to 'on' and she's all ready to go. You lock the case and you're on your way."

Duggan closed the lid of the attaché-case, turned the key in the lock and handed it to Fawley, who accepted it with some reluctance and dropped it into his pocket.

"Why did you pick me for this job?"

"Why not you? You've been wanting to strike a blow for the cause, haven't you?"

"Yes, but –"

"But what, Clyde?"

"When the bomb goes off there'll likely be people around. There'll be casualties."

"Sure there will, with any luck. Isn't that the object of the exercise?"

"I'm not sure I like it."

"We're not asking you to like it. Just do it. Like I said, that's an order. And if you really want to know, it wasn't me that picked you for this assignment; the decision was made higher up. I'm just carrying out my instructions."

Fawley stared at him in surprise. "You mean to say I was specially chosen for the job? By people in Ireland?"

"Yes."

"Why should they do that?"

"Your guess is as good as mine. Maybe they want to see how good you are. You ought to feel honoured, being trusted with something like this."

Fawley reflected that it was an honour he would gladly have done without. He wondered whether Duggan was being sarcastic.

"I hope," Duggan said; and there was a note of menace in his voice, "that you're not thinking of refusing. Because that would surely make us wonder whether you're really one of us at all and not some bloody undercover agent working for the anti-terrorist squad or what have you."

"You can't believe that," Fawley said.

"Oh, you'd be surprised what we can believe when we put our minds to it. And when we believe something like that we don't just let it go; we take measures. And a bit of knee-capping could be the least of them. Are you reading me, Clyde?"

Fawley was reading him with no difficulty at all. One false move and he would be in the dirt.

Duggan was watching him closely. "So what's it to be? Do you make the plant or do we have to wonder if we can really trust our American cousin?"

Fawley picked up the attaché-case. "Okay. I'll do it."

"Sensible man," Duggan said.

Fawley left the house by the same way he had come in. Molly was still in the kitchen and she glanced at the attaché-case.

"So you got what you came for?"

"I got this," Fawley said. "I didn't know it was what I was coming for until I got here. I guess you know what it is?"

"Oh, to be sure I do. You'll be very careful with it, won't you?"

"With something like this," Fawley said, "I'll be so careful you wouldn't believe."

He had almost reached the door when she said: "Goodbye, Clyde."

It was the way she said it that struck him; it was as though she were bidding him a last farewell; as if she did not expect to see him ever again. He turned and looked at her. She had a faintly mocking smile on her face as she looked back at him, and it made him uneasy. Did she, he asked himself, know something that he did not? Something it would have been to his advantage to know. Like what? Well, for instance, like the fact that he was never expected to return; that he was perhaps being set up, played for a sucker. But how? And why? Where would have been the point in it? So maybe he was just imagining things.

"Goodbye, Molly," he said.

He went straight back to Raven House, and when he had climbed the stairs he glanced up and saw Arthur Creech on the landing above leaning on the banister rail and gazing down at him.

"Good morning, Mr Fawley," Creech said. "You've been out and about, I see."

"Yes," Fawley said.

He was far from pleased to see Creech; he would have preferred to have reached his room without being observed. He felt oddly self-conscious with the attaché-case in his hand, as though it had to be evident to anyone who saw it that it contained a bomb. Which was, of course, quite ridiculous. In all probability Creech had not even noticed the case.

"I'd like to have a word with you if you've got the time to spare," Creech said.

He began to descend the stairs without waiting for an answer.

"Not now," Fawley said. "I've got things to do. Sorry. Another time perhaps."

He reached his own door before Creech could make it to the first floor, hurried into the room and closed the door behind him. He half expected Creech to come and knock on it, because he was not the sort of man to be easily put off; but he did not. Perhaps the word had not been very important. As likely as not it would simply have been another request for a loan, and maybe he had little expectation of success in that line.

Fawley looked around for somewhere to put the attaché-case and could find no better place than under the bed. Having put it there he sat down and thought about the situation. Of one thing he was certain; he would not, whatever happened, be delivering the bomb to Paddington Station. Even before his experience of the Regent Street bombing he had come to the conclusion that such methods of pressing the claims for a united Ireland were mean and despicable and that he would have no part in them.

So what ought he to do? The idea of going to the police came into his head and was dismissed. He was too deeply involved himself to take that course. But he could not simply leave the bomb under his bed indefinitely. Admittedly it was safe enough until the timing device had been set going, but it had to be disposed of somehow. The question was, how?

He decided to take a walk; perhaps in the open air his brain would come up with some answer to the problem. He encountered no one on the stairs or in the entrance hall when he left the house; but, unknown to him, his departure like his recent return did not go unnoticed. Creech had been hovering around on the upper landing and he spotted Fawley going down the stairs. He also made a mental note of the fact that the American was no longer carrying the attaché-case which he had brought in with him.

Arthur Creech was feeling piqued. The brusque manner in which Fawley had brushed aside his proposal of a little talk had annoyed him and he was in a vindictive mood and determined to get his own back on the younger man. If in so doing he should also make a bit of profit for himself, that would be bonus; for Creech was a man who had never been greatly bothered with the strict rules of ownership when the opportunity occurred to pick up any little piece of movable property. Indeed, he had at an earlier stage in his life supported himself entirely by petty thievery and had only given it up when advancing age had begun to mar his dexterity and a spell or two behind bars had convinced him that the flame was no longer worth the candle.

He had, however, retained sufficient of his former skill to make the entering of Fawley's room a simple operation, despite the fact that the door was locked. It took him scarcely any time to locate the attaché-case and discover that it also was locked. He wasted no time in trying to open it there and then, but let himself out of the room, relocked the door and made his way quickly to his own accommodation on the floor above. He was confident that no one had seen him either entering or leaving Fawley's room.

With the attaché-case resting on a table Creech began without haste to pick the lock. His curiosity was almost as strong as his cupidity; he had never entirely accepted the story that Fawley was residing in Raven House with the object of collecting material for a book and he believed that inside the attaché-case might be some clue to the true reason for his presence in that rather seedy and dilapidated building.

If Arthur Creech had been able to catch a glimpse of the contents of the case he might have made a pretty shrewd guess at one aspect of Fawley's activities, and he would certainly have had confirmation that they were not exclusively connected with the pursuit of creative writing. Unfortunately for him, however, he was destined never to obtain this knowledge. Just as curiosity killed the cat, so curiosity killed Arthur Creech. He was dead before he had completed the lifting of the lid.

*

Clyde Fawley heard the explosion. In fact he was already on his way back to Raven House, having come to the conclusion that the best way of disposing of the bomb would be to wait until nightfall and then carry it to one of the bridges spanning the Thames and drop it into the river. When he heard the explosion, muffled though it was by the buildings separating him from it, he had no doubt in his own mind that there would be no necessity to do anything with the attaché-case after all. Somehow or other it had been detonated prematurely.

He arrived at the house within minutes, even before the police and the emergency services, and he could see at once that he had been right about the location of the explosion. But there was something that puzzled him:

the main damage appeared to be not on the floor where his own room was situated but on the one above. He could see this because part of the outer wall had been blown out and there was rubble lying on the pavement and in the roadway. From the ground he could see into the house where the gap had been made, and he knew that he was looking into Arthur Creech's room.

As explosions went it had obviously been a small one. Most of the house was still intact, and but for that gaping hole in the upper wall it might have been impossible from the outside to tell that anything had happpened to it. But why should it have been Creech's room that had taken the brunt of the blast? It was too much to believe that there had been two bombs in the house.

He wasted no time speculating on this question, however, and he was just hurrying into the entrance hall when the first police car arrived; it must have been cruising in the area to have got there so quickly. He saw immediately that there was a body lying at the foot of the stairs, face downward and crumpled. He recognized the blonde hair and knew that it was Rita Woolley. He guessed that she had been going up to her room and had been thrown down the stairs by the force of the explosion.

She was not moving and the terrible possibility that she might be dead struck him like a blow. He knelt down and turned her gently over on to her back, supporting her head with his right arm. There was a gash in her forehead and a lot of blood on her face, but though her eyes were closed he discovered to his immense relief that she was breathing.

Two policemen from the patrol car had come into the house and one of them spoke to him.

"There'll be an ambulance here very soon. It'd be best not to move her, sir."

The other policeman was climbing the stairs. He called down from above: "There's a woman up here. She seems to be dead."

A little later the first ambulance arrived and Miss Woolley was taken over by more professional hands than Fawley's. She was carried out on a stretcher and loaded into the ambulance. He wished to go with her, but he knew that he would have been of no help to her and he needed to find out, if he could, just what had happened in the house during his brief absence.

There were more men in uniform on the scene now; all the emergency services doing their jobs; and as a helper he was superfluous. He went up to the second floor where most of the damage had been done and was able to identify the body of Miss Wills. Creech's room was a wreck, with much of the outer wall blown out. Creech himself was unrecognizable. Fortunately, no one else apart from the two women appeared to have been in the house at the time of the explosion.

Fawley's own room was not greatly damaged. The ceiling had been brought down and there was plaster lying on everything, but the walls and floor were intact. When he went in he glanced under the bed and saw that the attaché-case had gone. It took no great powers of deduction to guess who had taken it. He remembered Creech looking down at him when he arrived with the case in his hand, and there could be no doubt that the man had seen him go out again and then had broken into the room and purloined it. He must have taken it to his own room, picked the lock, opened it and tampered with the contents, setting off the bomb in the process.

When he had got this far in his reasoning Fawley came to a sudden halt, for he detected something wrong there. Creech had been a cunning old bird and he would have known at once that what he had on his hands was an explosive device. He would have had far too much sense to start tinkering with anything so potentially dangerous as that. And yet the fact remained that the bomb had gone off. So how? And why?

Well, maybe the mere opening of the attaché-case had been enough to trigger it off. But it should not have done so; and if it had, this fact opened up a whole new can of worms. It might have been accidental, of course, because bombs were tricky things at best; but a far more likely answer was that Duggan had fixed it so that the thing should blow up as soon as the case was opened.

And the person who should have opened it had not been Arthur Creech but none other than Clyde Fawley.

So!

Having reached this point Fawley did some more thinking and came to the conclusion that he really had been set up. Molly had indeed known something that he had not, and her parting word of goodbye had been intended as a last farewell, just as he had suspected. All that stuff about setting the timing device and taking the attaché-case to Paddington Station had just been so much eyewash. It had never been intended that he should put it in the left-luggage locker, and maybe there were no such lockers; one way or the other, it made no difference. It had all been an elaborate arrangement to get rid of him; he saw that now. He was to have been liquidated, blown away, wasted, as the expression was.

But why?

Why, granted that they wanted to get rid of him, should they have gone to so much trouble to accomplish what a single bullet in the heart would have done so much more simply and cheaply? And then he remembered that Duggan had said that the order had come from higher up; so perhaps the people in Ireland regarded him for some reason or other as an embarrassment of which they wished to disencumber themselves. And they would not wish to risk alienating their supporters in America who were supplying them with arms and ammunition and good hard cash; so the death of a young American volunteer had to be made to appear accidental. A lot of IRA men had been blown up by their own bombs; it was one of the hazards of active service. So he, Clyde Fawley, would have died a hero's death and a lot of people on the other side of the Atlantic would have been proud of him, never suspecting that he had in fact been murdered by those he had tried to help.

It fitted. Oh, it really fitted.

But he, by a completely unforeseen chance, had escaped; and Arthur Creech had been blown to bits and poor inoffensive Miss Wills was dead and Rita Woolley injured, just how badly he still did not know.

In Fawley's mind there was a growing anger; anger with Duggan and Connolly and Molly and all those unknown men who had authority over them and could order such despicable crimes to be committed. He had a burning desire to strike back at them, but there was a sense of frustration because he could see no way of doing it.

*

He had to answer a lot of questions from the police. Miss Woolley was in no condition to be interrogated and he was the nearest person they had to an eye-witness, even though he had not been in the house at the time of the explosion. He wondered whether they suspected him of being in any way involved; but there was no reason why they should and he knew that it was only a sense of guilt that made him read a deeper meaning in the questions than was superficially apparent.

It was evening before he was able to visit Miss Woolley in hospital. She was in a private room and the only way he could gain admittance was by claiming that he was her fiancé.

Raven House had been evacuated, temporarily at least, until repairs could be carried out and it was declared structurally safe. Fawley had moved his luggage to a cheap hotel and had given his new address to the police in case they should wish to contact him. It had been their suggestion.

Miss Woolley was pleased to see him. She was not looking well; it would have been strange if she had been. She had a broken arm and internal injuries and she would probably have a permanent scar on her forehead to remind her of what had happened. But it could have been worse; she was alive and would get well again, and that was all that mattered.

"It was nice of you to come," she said.

"They would have had to put up barbed wire to stop me," Fawley told her. "And incidentally, you'd better know that we're engaged."

"Engaged!"

"If we hadn't been they wouldn't have let me in. You're not allowed to see just anybody until you're better."

She gave a wan smile. "Well, you're certainly not just anybody, are you?" And then: "It's a funny thing, you know; I can't even remember when you proposed."

"It'll come to you," Fawley said.

She asked about Miss Wills. Fawley hesitated. He was not sure whether it would be advisable to tell her the truth; it might upset her. But she settled the question for him.

"She's dead, isn't she?"

Fawley did not deny it.

"I was going up to speak to her," Miss Woolley said. "She called down to me from the floor above, saying she had something to tell me. I shall never know what it was now. I was still on the first-floor landing when there was this almighty explosion. It must have knocked me off my feet and thrown me down the lower flight of stairs into the hall. I don't remember anything else."

"I'm just thankful you weren't killed," Fawley said. "I'd never have forgiven myself for that. It's bad enough Miss Wills being dead, and –"

He saw that she was staring at him in astonishment. "Whatever do you mean, you wouldn't have forgiven yourself? What would there have been to forgive? Surely you don't feel you were in any way to blame? It had nothing to do with you, did it?"

Fawley saw that he had made a slip of the tongue and he hastened to repair the damage. "No, of course not. It's just that somehow I feel guilty for not being there."

"But you couldn't have done anything. You might have been killed yourself."

"That's true."

"Well, then –"

He did not stay long. He had been told not to tire the patient. As he was leaving she said:

"I won't hold you to it, you know."

"Hold me to what?"

She gave a kind of nervous giggle. "The engagement."

"Oh, that," he said. "Well, I don't know. Maybe I'd like you to. Hold me to it, I mean."

She looked suddenly so radiant that he wondered whether it had been a wise thing to say. Though the words had been spoken lightly it was obvious that she had taken them in all seriousness. And the truth of the matter was, he just could not be sure whether he had meant her to or not.

Chapter Eleven – SMALL TRIUMPH

Fawley waited until the evening of the following day before paying a visit to the builder's yard. He had had another interview with the police, but he was satisfied that they had no suspicions regarding his involvement with the explosion at Raven House. They seemed to be acting on the theory that Arthur Creech had been making a bomb in his room and had accidentally caused the explosion which had killed him and Miss Wills. They wanted Fawley to tell them all he knew about Creech. He did his best, but it was little enough; he knew only what Miss Wills had told him, having himself only recently come to live in the house and having had very few contacts with the man.

"So you don't know if he was involved in any terrorist activities?"

"No," Fawley said. "I'd have thought it unlikely. He didn't seem that kind of man."

"What kind of man was he?"

"A bit down-at-heel. Short of money, I'd say."

"What makes you think that?"

"He tried to borrow ten pounds off me the first time we spoke to each other. He also asked for a glass of whisky, but I hadn't got any."

"You think he drank?"

"It's possible. I just don't know. The fact is I know practically nothing about the man."

The odd thing was that he had the impression that the police knew far more about Arthur Creech than he did. Perhaps they were only asking the questions as a matter of form.

He took the pistol with him when he went to the builder's yard, and as usual he went to the back door of the house. It was Molly who opened the door, and she gave him a curious sort of look; a trifle wary, as though she scented trouble.

"Oh, so it's you."

"Weren't you expecting me?" Fawley asked.

"Why should we be expecting you?"

"I thought you'd be wanting a report. On my mission, you know. The bomb."

"Ah!" she said, still wary. "That!"

"Yes, that. Aren't you going to let me in?"

She stood aside then, making room for him to walk into the kitchen. She told him to follow her and she conducted him to a room he had never been in before. It was fairly large, but there was not much space in which to move around because it appeared to have been used as a dump for second-hand furniture and junk of various kinds. There was a pretty thread-bare carpet on the floor and there were four armchairs and a dilapidated sofa and a chest of drawers with the worm in it and quite an assortment of small side-tables.

Duggan was sitting in one of the armchairs and Connolly was on the sofa with his feet up, smoking a pipe. By the fact that they showed no great surprise at seeing him Fawley could tell that they already knew something had gone wrong with their plan. They had probably read about the Raven House explosion in the papers and had learned that the wrong man had been killed.

"Well, look who's here," Connolly said. "We was just talking about you."

"Is that so? I hope you found it an interesting subject for discussion."

"Oh, sure. We was asking ourselves how come we've had no report of an explosion at Paddington Station."

Connolly was grinning at him, and it infuriated Fawley. He felt an urge to rush at Connolly and wipe the grin off his face with a solid punch to the jaw; but that would have been the wrong way to handle the situation.

"You know damn well how come," he said. "There was never meant to be any explosion at Paddington. I was never expected to get that far."

"So you've figured that out, have you?" Duggan said, watching him closely.

"You bet I've figured it out."

Duggan nodded. "What we don't understand is how it happened the way it did. What went wrong?"

"You mean wrong for you? It's simple. I left the case in my room and while I was out of the house a man named Creech who used to live on the floor above broke in and took it. He must have opened it and it blew up in his face."

"Now that," Duggan said, "is something we just didn't think of. A thief in the house."

"A nice harmless old lady was killed too." Fawley was having difficulty in containing his anger. The off-hand manner in which Duggan and Connolly appeared to be treating the matter infuriated him. They seemed unconcerned with the death and injury caused by the bomb and to be interested only in the reason why the plot had misfired. "There was a girl who was badly hurt as well."

"A friend of yours?" Duggan inquired, with a sneer.

"Yes, a friend of mine."

"You shouldn't have got yourself mixed up with such people. You were warned."

"I don't give a damn about being warned. And by God, when it comes to a question of friends I guess I'd do better looking for them anywhere but amongst you lot. A fine set of bastards you turned out to be."

Duggan was cool. "Don't let it upset you." He spoke to the girl. "Look, Moll, why don't you go and make some coffee, huh?"

She took it as an order and went out of the room.

"Sit down, Clyde," Duggan said. "I think we'd better talk things over. There's a bit of a problem here."

Fawley knew what the problem was and he doubted whether any amount of talking would solve it. He was not sure if it had been wise to come there; it had been rather like walking into the spider's parlour. He had had some vague idea of settling things with these men, but he had known there could only be one way of settling a matter of this kind: with a gun. He ought to shoot the bastards; he had every right to do so, because they had intended killing him; but when it came to the point he found himself incapable of hauling out the pistol and shooting them in cold blood. It was just not on. And he was furious with himself because it was not; he saw it as a weakness in his character.

"Okay," he said, "let's talk." He sat down in an armchair from which he could keep an eye on both men and also the door. "Why did you try to kill me?"

Duggan gave a shrug. "It's like I told you; we had orders."

"From Ireland?"

"Yes; a man came."

"But I don't get it. Why would they want me killed?"

"It was because of the interception of the arms shipment."

"But I had nothing to do with that. I told you."

"I know you told us. But you would, wouldn't you? You were bound to deny it. Anyway, they were suspicious of you right from the start. Grady had doubts about you and there was this feeling that you might be an infiltrator, an undercover agent."

"So why did they let me come? They could have refused."

"Maybe they thought it best to have you where they could keep an eye on you. And besides, there was pressure, so I believe."

"But good God, man; where's the proof that I've done anything to betray you? All you've got is suspicion and some pretty thin circumstantial evidence that wouldn't be enough to hang a dog."

"Well now," Duggan said, "that's as may be. But if we always waited for cast-iron proof that a man was a traitor we'd be in real trouble, sure we would. In this game you've got to be quick off the mark if you want to stay alive."

"So you'll sentence a man to death on nothing better than suspicion?"

"We do what we think best," Duggan said.

"Well, you made a real cock-up of this one, didn't you?"

"The rub of the green. You can't win 'em all."

"You were lucky," Connolly said. "But it looks like you didn't have the sense to make use of your luck. You should've taken off and kept running. Instead you came back here. Did you want to make it easy for us?"

"I don't get you," Fawley said.

"Ah, come off it. You're not that simple. You know as well as we do there's a job not finished."

"Do you mean you still intend to kill me?"

"Why not? Nothing's changed. And here you are, come like a lamb to the slaughter."

"Not quite," Fawley said; and he pulled out the Browning self-loader.

They seemed unimpressed. Connolly gave a jeering laugh.

"Are you sure you know how to use that shooter?"

"For your information," Fawley said in a hard cold voice, "I could shoot the nose off your face if I wanted to. I was handling guns when I was knee-high to a grasshopper. So don't do anything stupid, because there's nothing I'd like better at this moment than to drill you both."

It stopped the laughter. He could see that they believed him and it was giving them food for thought.

"Now don't do anything hasty," Duggan said. "Maybe we can do a deal."

"And maybe I'm the one that's going to do a deal. With the police."

"The police, is it? And you said you were no traitor."

"Now look who's talking," Fawley said. "When it comes to treachery I guess you could teach me a thing or two."

He thought of getting up and leaving then. Nothing had been resolved, and though he had talked about going to the police he was not at all sure he would do it; but there was nothing more to be gained by argument. He was about to get up from the chair when the door opened and Molly came in with a tray on which were four steaming mugs of coffee.

She looked at the gun in Fawley's hand but said nothing.

"Serve the guest first," Duggan said.

"I don't want any coffee," Fawley said. But she was already coming towards him and there was no way of stopping her.

She came to a halt in front of him, the tray balanced on the palm of her left hand.

"Take it."

"No. I don't want any."

"Oh, but you do," she said. And then she picked up one of the mugs with her right hand and flung the contents in his face.

He was temporarily blinded by the hot liquid and in some pain. But there were only a few seconds in which he had to endure the pain, because one of the men must have come at him very quickly and something considerably harder than a clenched fist gave him a crack on the head before he could get his sight back. Whatever the instrument was, it put the snuffers on him pretty effectively and for a while any further part he took in the proceedings was of a totally passive nature.

When he was able once again to take notice of what was going on around him he discovered that he was still sitting in the armchair and that he was suffering from just about the worst headache he could remember. He could have used a couple of aspirins and a glass of water, but he doubted whether it would have been of any use putting in a request for such small medical aid.

He had no way of telling how long he had been knocked out, but there had certainly been time for someone to do a very good job of trussing him up. His wrists were tied behind his back and his ankles had also been bound together with a length of strong cord. Quite apart from the pain in his head he was in some physical discomfort, and quite involuntarily he gave a low moan.

The sound revealed the fact that he had regained consciousness and he became aware that Duggan had approached the chair and was looking down at him.

"So you're awake, sonny boy. How're you feeling?"

"Like hell," Fawley said. He could see Duggan clearly enough and there was no double vision, so he guessed he was not suffering from concussion. Which was some small comfort; though how long he would live to enjoy that comfort was an open question. His eyes were watering slightly, but this was probably the effect of the coffee. "What did you hit me with?"

"I didn't. It was Sean."

"Well, what did he use?"

Connolly answered for himself. He was standing by the mantelpiece and still smoking his foul pipe. "It was this." He stooped and picked up a shovel from the hearth. "It did a nice clean job; no messing. You went out like a light."

Fawley was thankful he had not used the poker, which might well have inflicted more serious damage. Connolly was grinning, as though highly pleased with himself.

"You shouldn't threaten people with guns. It isn't nice."

"I should have drilled the pair of you when I had the chance." Fawley was angry with himself for having let the girl get near him; he should have guessed she might take a hand.

She was sitting on the sofa now, very much at ease, looking at him again with that faintly mocking expression which she seemed to reserve for him.

"Ah well," Connolly said, "that's the way it goes; you don't take the chance when you have it and maybe it never comes again. It's a bad old world."

Fawley wondered what they were planning to do with him. It was obvious that they were not intending to kill him there; otherwise they would already have done so; there would have been nothing to gain by delaying it. On the other hand it was also obvious that they had no intention of letting him go.

Duggan seemed to read the question in his mind. He said: "We'll be leaving when it gets dark."

"Leaving for where?"

"You'll see. Just be patient."

He had to be patient for three hours. The time passed slowly and uncomfortably. His head throbbed and his limbs felt stiff. There was always one man or the girl in his room with him, just to make sure he made no escape. There was little conversation; there seemed to be nothing much to say.

Once he said: "You're making a big mistake, you know. You have no reason for killing me."

It was Connolly who was with him at the time and he just laughed. "Since when did anybody need a reason for killing anybody else?"

He could think of no good answer to that. There were people all over the world who were killing other people for no good reason at all. It was human nature.

It was soon after ten o'clock when the two men carried him out into the yard. They had gagged him first with a piece of cloth and he could make no more than muffled sounds which would not have brought anyone to his assistance from a distance of twenty feet. And he certainly could have used some assistance.

The Cortina was standing in the yard and they put him in the boot. They had emptied it first, but it was still fairly cramped for a man of his size. The girl had remained in the house, so he gathered that she was not coming along with them. There was no need for her to do so; Duggan and Connolly were capable of handling what there was to do.

They closed the lid and he was in utter darkness, the air reeking of petrol and rubber. He had a sudden terror of suffocating and he had to fight the hysteria that threatened to take control of him. He heard the doors slam and the whirring of the starter and he could tell when the car turned into the roadway outside the yard; but after that he had no means of knowing where they were or where they were going. He knew he was being taken to some place where Duggan and Connolly could conveniently kill him and dispose of the body, but there was nothing he could do about it; the position was hopeless.

But after a few minutes had passed he told himself that this was a spineless attitude to take. There must be something he could do, something he could at least try. He was damned if he would give in without some kind of a fight for life.

The essential necessity was to free his wrists; all else would stem from that and if he failed to do so there really was little hope. And what was the classic method of cutting through one's bonds? By chafing them on something sharp or abrasive, of course. In this particular case the problem was to find the sharp or abrasive object in utter darkness and in the strictly limited area of the boot of a car. But perhaps there would be somewhere a projecting piece of metal, a bit of rough welding or something of that sort which would serve the purpose.

With considerable difficulty and a certain amount of pain he managed to shift his position, searching with his fingers for the required cutting edge. After about ten minutes of this activity he was short of breath under the gag and running with sweat. He rested, breathing hard through his nose and almost choked by the cloth in his mouth. It was useless, a waste of effort, and the only abrasions he was getting were on the exposed parts of his skin. He might as well give up and just wait for what was coming to him.

Nevertheless, after a while he started again, twisting his body into all manner of contortions in order to move it around in the boot. Again there was no useful result; he could discover nothing that would conceivably cut the bonds and he was sweating more heavily than ever.

He rested again; it really was hopeless and he had better reconcile himself to the fact. Why distress himself further in a vain attempt to get free?

He moved his hands in order to ease himeself into a less uncomfortable position and was suddenly aware that the cord binding his wrists had loosened slightly. All his twisting and turning in the vain search for some object to sever the bonds had had the unexpected result of presenting the possibility of getting free of them in quite another way. He started to work at it, and what with the loosening of the cord and the lubricating effect of the sweat on his skin he was able before long to slip his right hand out of the constricting bonds.

It was a triumph, though a small one; for he was still deep in trouble. But now there was a glimmer of hope where before there had been none. With his hands free he was able to remove the gag and the feeling of being suffocated lessened. He loosed his ankles and did what he could in his narrow prison to ease the stiffness out of his limbs, for he knew that everything depended on the quickness of his movements when eventually the lid of the boot was lifted.

What he needed most was some kind of weapon, and he groped around in search of one. A wrench overlooked when the boot had been emptied would have been ideal; a jack or a wheel-brace or even a spanner would have been acceptable; but there was nothing, nothing at all. He regretted the loss of the pistol; with that in his hand he would have had little to fear.

The Cortina was still going ahead. Now and then it came to a halt and he thought perhaps they had reached the end of the journey; but he could hear other vehicles and he guessed that they were merely being held up by the traffic. He might have hammered on the lid of the boot and shouted for help, but he felt sure it would have been useless and he did not even try it. Instead, he remained silent and inactive, conserving his energy and waiting for the moment when he would need all his strength and ingenuity if he were to save himself from extinction.

Chapter Twelve – VISITOR

The journey seemed interminable to the prisoner in the boot, but as all things must it eventually came to an end. The last part of the way must have been over a very rough sort of track, as he could tell from all the bumping and swaying which added to his discomfort; but he guessed that the pay-off was near and he braced himself mentally as well as physically for the crucial moment that was soon to come.

The car came to a stop and the engine died. He waited, tense, alert. He heard the shuffle of feet on rough ground and then the metallic sound of the catch on the boot being released. The lid went up and there was a little light to take the place of the total darkness in which he had been immersed for the duration of the journey. It was not much but it was enough to reveal the shadowy figure of Sean Connolly standing there. There was no sign of Duggan.

Fawley moved quickly, like a spring released. He was up in a moment and he took a jump and hit Connolly with the full weight of his body. Connolly fell over backwards with Fawley on top of him and he made a grunting sound as the breath was driven out of him. But Fawley was up again on the instant, for there was still Duggan to reckon with. He aimed a kick at Connolly's head and had the satisfaction of feeling the toe of his shoe make contact and hearing Connolly give a cry of pain. And then he was running away from the car as fast as he could go, not knowing where he was heading but certain that at all costs he had to get away.

He heard a shout and recognized Duggan's voice: "Stop right there or I'll shoot."

He glanced back and could see Duggan standing by the car. The headlights were on and Duggan was silhouetted against the background of light while all around there was a shadowy emptiness, except where the beam of the heads revealed an uneven landscape curiously like the surface of the moon.

Fawley did not check his pace but ran on. He heard the crack of the gun and the sound of a bullet smacking into the stony ground close to his pounding feet. There followed a second shot and a third, but they were not on target and there were no more after that. Duggan was probably having difficulty in seeing what he was aiming at in the gloom and had come to the conclusion that he was simply wasting bullets.

Fawley glanced back again and saw Duggan and Connolly getting into the car, and he put on a spurt because he could guess what their intention was. He was going as hard as he could and able to see very little of what was ahead of him when he put his right foot in a hole and fell heavily. He was up again quickly enough, but he had twisted his ankle and the run had become a limp. A moment later the headlights picked him up and he could hear the Cortina accelerating in pursuit.

It was apparent to him now that the place he had been brought to was some kind of disused quarry or old excavation for gravel. There was a sort of cliff in the distance revealed by the lights, but even if he could have reached it before the Cortina overtook him he was not sure he could have climbed it, especially with Duggan and Connolly taking pot-shots at him as he did so. He was in a fix and he knew it.

The car was almost on him as he turned to face it. It did not slacken speed, but he managed to leap to one side as it came at him and it went by and made a fast U-turn and accelerated again. There was no way he could stay ahead of it by running, so he tried the same trick as before and the offside front wing missed him by inches. He staggered and fell, and his right hand came into contact with a large stone. He grasped it and stood up, not trying to get away any more because there was no chance of doing so; in the end the car must catch him, run over him, kill him. So he stood and waited, poised and ready, the heavy stone in his hand.

He let the car get to within a few yards of him before throwing the stone; he had to get it right the first time, since he might not have a second chance. And he did get it right; the stone, which must have weighed three or four pounds at least, hit the windscreen and shattered it, and in the same instance he flung himself to the left.

The wing caught him a glancing blow and it hurt like hell but it threw him clear. He went down on his hands and knees and he could see the car careering on as if out of control. It went on for about thirty or forty yards and then suddenly it was not there; it had vanished. One moment it had been in full view and the next moment there was nothing to be seen; it had completely disappeared.

It was unbelievable. Fawley got to his feet and he still could not believe it. And yet there was no way of not believing it if he could credit his senses; for the fact was indisputable: the car had gone, the lights had gone, the sound of the engine had gone.

So how had it happened?

He started walking in the direction in which the Cortina had gone, and now there was only some sickly moonlight filtering through the clouds to reveal his surroundings and it was impossible to see anything at all clearly. He walked slowly and warily, and it was as well for him that he did, for suddenly he found himself at the edge of a pit and another step would have carried him headlong over the brink.

He came to an abrupt halt and looked down, and at this moment the clouds thinned slightly to let the light of the sliver of moon shine through, so that it was possible to glimpse the murky surface of stagnant water some ten or fifteen feet below him. As he stared at it some bubbles rose from the depths and he knew where the Cortina was lying.

There was no sign of either of the two men, and he came to the conclusion that they were trapped in the car. By this time they would surely be dead. The stone had done it; it had blinded the driver and he had not seen the danger ahead but had allowed the car to speed on to its destruction.

Fawley could muster no regret; if he had not done what he had Duggan and Connolly would still have been alive but he would almost certainly have been dead. And when it came to a choice between his life and theirs he was selfish enough to opt for his own. It was probable that his body would have ended up in this very pit or another like it, suitably weighted down with some pieces of old iron or a rock or two if things had gone according to plan. It might have been years before the skeleton had been found; it might have lain there undetected for ever.

He turned and walked away, limping a little, sore on the right buttock where the car had hit him and still with a throbbing ache in the head, but glad to be alive. For when it came to the point that was the great thing: to be alive.

*

He got back to his hotel in the early hours of the morning and the night porter looked at him as if he had been something nasty that the cat had deposited on the doorstep. And well he might, since Fawley was dirty and unshaven and haggard, and there were coffee stains on his shirt and jacket.

It had taken him some time to find the right road. He had discovered later that he was in Hertfordshire, some distance from London; and he had walked for a few miles and then thumbed a lift in a lorry taking a load of vegetables to market. The driver had been interested in his condition and Fawley had told him that he had had an accident with a motor-cycle. He doubted whether the man had been convinced, but it would have been madness to have told him anything approaching the truth. He had travelled the last part of the journey by tube and then again on foot. He was happy to be back; he could so easily never have made it.

He went up to his room and had a bath and crawled into bed, feeling bruised and sore and generally pretty hard done by. But it could have been worse.

Although he was thoroughly worn out he found it difficult to get to sleep; his brain went ticking on like a piece of cheap clockwork, and all that had happened to him in the past ten hours or so came back to him in a kind of action replay time after time after time. But finally he dropped off and had the same programme in a more garbled dream version, a horror movie played on the video recorder of his subconscious mind.

He woke late, still with the lingering remains of the headache and with a body that felt as though it had been on the losing end of an all-in wrestling bout. But he got up and swallowed some aspirins and gradually the stiffness began to wear off. He left the hotel and found a café and drank several cups of coffee while he thought about the situation and tried to figure out what it would be best to do.

Undoubtedly the correct course of action would have been to go to the police and lay before them a complete account of what had happened. They could hardly hold him responsible for the deaths of Duggan and Connolly; he had acted entirely in self-defence because they were doing their damnedest to murder him. But of course there was more to it than that, a whole lot more. There was involvement with the IRA for a start; there was the matter of the bomb in Raven House and there was the nasty business of the robbery at the post office: all these bits and pieces might float to the surface if he started stirring up the mud and he could find himself in big trouble.

So maybe, on consideration, it would be wise not to tell the police about the nocturnal incident in Hertfordshire.

He thought of Molly and wondered whether he ought to pay her a visit and tell her what had happened. She would certainly be worrying because they should have returned long before this.

But then it occurred to him that he was under no obligation to relieve her anxiety. What had she ever done for him except throw a cup of hot coffee in his face? She had been as much involved in the attempt on his life as the two men and a bit of worry was little enough in the way of retribution. Besides which, if he were to carry the news to her of the way Duggan and Connolly had died she might try to kill him by way of revenge. She might not be too bothered about the loss of Connolly, but Duggan had been her man and she was bound to be enraged by the news of his death.

So on the whole it might be best not to give Molly any information either.

He wondered how much she knew. Had she been told where the men were proposing to take him for the killing job? Probably. And if so she would have a good idea of where to go looking for them. But of one thing he felt reasonably certain: she would not call in the police; she had too much to hide.

To kill time he travelled up to the West End and wandered around the National Gallery and had lunch in an Italian restaurant in Soho. As soon as the evening papers came out he bought one and scanned it for any news of the discovery of two men drowned in a car in an old gravel pit. But there was nothing of the kind and he felt a sense of relief.

Later he paid another visit to Rita Woolley in the hospital. She noticed the bruise on his temple.

"What happened to your head, Clyde?"

"I knocked it on a door."

"Are you sure you haven't been in a fight?"

"Of course. What makes you think that?"

"I don't know. You look tired. Sometimes I worry about you."

"Well, it's good to know somebody does," Fawley said; and he meant it; it gave him a warm feeling inside. "But there's no need. You're the one we should be worrying about."

"Oh, I'll be all right. I'm getting on fine. It was nice of you to come. Wasting your valuable time and everything."

"Valuable!" he said. "Now who's kidding?" He took her hand in both of his. "Anyway, I'll always have time for you."

It pleased her; he could see that. It even brought the moisture to her eyes.

"You're sweet, Clyde," she said. "And I love you."

"I love you too, Rita," Fawley said. And he half believed it was the truth.

*

He had been back in his hotel room for about fifteen minutes when somebody knocked on the door. He opened it and saw Molly standing outside. She immediately brushed past him into the room and after a slight hesitation he closed the door.

"So they didn't kill you," Molly said.

She was wearing jeans and a black jumper and a short leather jacket and he had the impression that she was under the influence of some powerful emotion which she was only with difficulty managing to hold in check.

"It doesn't look like it, does it?" he said.

"So what happened?"

Even now he wondered whether it would be wise to tell her. "Maybe you'd better sit down."

He indicated a chair and she looked at it and he thought she was going to refuse, but then she sat down abruptly, though she did not relax but remained rigidly upright, as if she had a rod in her back.

"So you knew they meant to kill me?"

"Well, of course I did. Why else would they have been taking you away in the boot? For a joy-ride?"

"It was hardly that for me."

"But you're still alive. I don't understand. How did you manage it?"

"I did a Houdini act."

"You mean you got free?"

"Yes. I managed to slip a hand out of the cord on my wrists and after that it was simple."

"When did you do it?"

"During the journey."

"But you'd still be in the boot. How did you get out?"

"Connolly opened it when we got to our destination. I took him by surprise; he wasn't expecting me to jump out at him like a jack-in-the-box and he wasn't ready for it."

"Are you telling me that's how you got away? That you just knocked him down and ran off?"

"I'm here, am I not?"

She stared at him through narrowed eyes. "But they haven't come back. So there's more to it than that, isn't there? There has to be."

Fawley could see that there was no point in denying it; she would not have believed him. "Yes; there's more to it."

"Tell me," she said.

He told her. She listened in silence until he had completed the account. Then she said in a low tense voice:

"So you killed them?"

"No; they killed themselves."

"If you hadn't thrown a rock through the windscreen they would never have gone into the pit."

"It was done in self-defence. They were trying to run me down. What would you expect me to do? Lie down and let them run over me?"

"Damn you!" she said; and she seemed to be spitting venom. "Do you think I'd give two pins what happened to you, you Yankee bastard. It was Pat who mattered to me, nobody but him. And you killed him."

"Well, I'm not going to say I'm sorry," Fawley said. "I guess he had it coming to him."

He turned away from her, having no desire to pursue the argument. It was done and it could never be undone, and that was that. She would have to accept the fact and live with it as best she could.

He heard a sound behind him and knew that it had been a mistake to turn his back on her even for an instant. He should have known better than to take his eye off her, should have known that she could not be trusted; because she was as much of a killer as Duggan or Connolly had been.

He swung round quickly now and saw her coming at him, her face contorted with hate and a knife in her right hand. It was the kind of knife you found in modern kitchens; bright steel, serrated along the cutting edge, razor-sharp, about ten inches long, tapering to a point. It must have been concealed under the leather jacket, perhaps in a pocket or sheath specially made to take it.

She was screaming at him like a crazy woman: "Bastard! Bastard! Bastard!" But there was nothing crazy about her handling of the knife; she used it in the professional manner, not with a wild over-arm lunge but with the lethal upward thrust that would miss the ribs and reach for the heart.

Fawley had swift reactions but he moved only just in time. He swayed to the right and the blade ripped his shirt and he felt it slide across the flesh between hip and rib, tearing the skin and marking him with a red line of blood.

She fell against him, carried forward by the sheer force of the blow, and he hit her with a fierce right uppercut that took her on the chin and knocked her down. She still had the knife in her hand and he stood on her wrist and pinned it to the floor. He stooped and prised the knife from her fingers and touched her throat with the point, which was stained with his own blood.

"Cool it," he said.

She stared up at him with the venom and hatred in her eyes, but she knew she was beaten and she cooled it.

He let her get up, and she stood there breathing hard and rubbing her chin where he had hit her. He glanced down at his side and could see the blood staining his shirt.

"You'd better go now," he said. "You've done enough damage for one day."

"No," she said. "Not nearly enough."

"Well, get to hell out of it, anyway."

She scowled at him. "Don't think you'll get away, you bastard. I may have failed this time, but if I don't get you they will. They'll be looking for you wherever you go. Because it's not only the treachery now; it's the two good men you killed. They won't forget that."

He could guess whom she meant by "they". They were the people who had given the order to Duggan and Connolly. He hoped she was wrong, but he feared she could well be right.

When she had gone he took off the torn shirt and cleaned the wound. It was nothing, a shallow scratch no more than two inches long. He had some adhesive dressings in the first-aid-kit he carried around with him and he patched himself up with one of these. A few more days and he would be as good as new – if nothing worse happened to him.

But he could see that it was time to return to the States; he had business there which needed to be sorted out and there was nothing more for him to do on this side of the Atlantic. His connection with the IRA was broken and would never be restored.

*

When he told Rita Woolley he was going back to America her face clouded.

"So this is the last time I'll see you?"

"Only for the present. It's not goodbye for ever, you know."

"I wish I could be sure of that."

"You can. I promise."

"No," she said; and there was a note of hopelessness in her voice. "You may say that now; you may even think it; but I'll never see you again. I know."

He tried to brush the suggestion aside. "Oh, sure you will. I'll be back."

But he could tell that she did not believe it. There was an emptiness in her eyes that was almost like despair. It was as though she saw all her hopes, all her dreams fading into nothingness.

Fawley kissed her and she clung to him for a moment with her good arm. But it was not enough and he knew it. Perhaps he could have made his words of assurance more convincing if he had really believed them himself.

Chapter Thirteen – FOURTH TIME

It was evening when Fawley arrived in New York and he went straight from the airport to his uncle's house on Riverside Drive. He had sent no message ahead of him to give warning of his decision to return to the States and it came as a complete surprise to Daniel O'Higgins when he appeared.

O'Higgins was not alone; he had his three closest friends, McNulty, Cooney and Mitchell, with him. They were all surprised to see Fawley, but they gave him a hearty welcome. Fawley was not at all pleased to see them; he had been hoping to find his uncle alone; there were things he had to say that could not be said in the presence of the other men.

But they showed no inclination to leave; they knew that he had been over to Ireland to give his services for the Republican cause and they wanted to hear all about it. To all their eager questions he made evasive answers, but it was not easy to fob them off. To them he was a kind of hero, a man who had been at the heart of the conflict, had seen what it was really like over there.

Mitchell slapped him on the shoulder. "I want you to know we're proud of you, young man. I guess they were glad to have you with them, huh? They made you welcome, I guess."

"They made me welcome."

"It figures. An American volunteer. Made them feel like they're not alone in the struggle."

"Perhaps."

"Can you tell us what you did? Any operations you took part in."

"I'm sorry," Fawley said. "It wouldn't do, you know."

McNulty tapped the side of his nose. "We understand. Military secrets."

A meaning glance passed between the three men, as much as to say that they needed no convincing of the importance of absolute discretion in such matters.

"Can't be too careful even among friends," Cooney said. "We know what can happen when things leak out."

Fawley guessed that he was referring to the interception of the arms shipment and he sensed a hint of uneasiness among them. He wondered what they would have said if he had told them that he had been under suspicion because of that; their hero suspected of being a traitor.

He was glad when they took their leave; it had become difficult to keep up the pretence that he was still as fervent as ever in support of the cause. They must have been wondering why he was no longer on the other side of the Atlantic, why his stay had been so brief. But they seemed to hesitate to put the question bluntly to him.

But when they were gone O'Higgins was less inhibited. He demanded point blank:

"What's wrong, Clyde?"

"Wrong?"

"Ah, come on, boy; you know what I mean. You were supposed to stay over there longer than this. What made you decide to come home?"

Fawley had been trying to figure out the best way of telling O'Higgins; he had thought about it on the flight from London, but he had come to no conclusion. Whatever he said, whichever way he put it, it was not going to please Uncle Danny.

"I've changed my mind," he said.

O'Higgins stared at him. "Changed your mind! What in hell is that supposed to mean?"

"It means I've finished with all that Irish business. I should never have gone. I was a fool to let you persuade me that it would be a glorious thing to do."

O'Higgins was astonished; he seemed unable to believe what he had heard. "You mean you're throwing your hand in? Giving up the cause."

"The cause!" Fawley spoke with disgust. "What cause? It was a dream, don't you understand? Just a dream. A dream of madness."

O'Higgins shook his head vehemently. "You're wrong. You don't know what you're talking about."

"Oh, but I do," Fawley said. "You're the one who's got it all wrong. What do you know about the situation over there? What do you know about the British people? Have you ever been to England?"

"You bet your sweet life I haven't. I wouldn't set foot on that soil. I wouldn't demean myself by even speaking to those murdering bastards."

"Of course you wouldn't. And do you know why? Because you're bigoted. You know nothing. You don't even want to know."

O'Higgins sat down in an armchair and regarded his nephew in a puzzled sort of way. Then he said:

"Somebody's been getting at you, Clyde; that's what it is. They've been feeding you propaganda."

"Nobody's got at me and nobody's been feeding me any propaganda. I know what propaganda is; I ought to; I've had enough from you."

"I've never told you anything but the truth."

"Maybe you thought it was the truth; I'll give you the benefit of the doubt. Maybe you believed it all yourself. And so you made me believe. But not any more; never again. I started doubting very soon after I got over to the other side; and the doubts grew; they grew because of what I saw, what I experienced. And if I'd needed anything else to convince me how wrong I'd been it would have come when they tried to kill me."

O'Higgins was so startled by these words that he shot bolt upright in the chair. "Kill you! Who tried to kill you?"

"The IRA boys, the Provos. Who else?"

"But why? You must have it wrong. It doesn't make sense. You were there to help them."

"That's what I thought. But they never really wanted me, you know. I was just so much garbage getting in their way. That was why they shunted me off to London, made me join a cell. And then they got this crazy idea that I was the one who informed about the arms shipment."

O'Higgins stared at him. "They suspected you of that?"

"Oh, yes. And by their kind of logic it meant that I had to be removed. Permanently. Do you know how they planned to do that?"

O'Higgins sighed heavily. "You'd better tell me."

"Okay, I will," Fawley said. He had been standing, walking restlessly about the room, that large oak-panelled library where he had first met Michael Grady, the dried-up little Irishman whom he had regarded as a hero. Now, however, he sat down in one of the leather-upholstered armchairs. "I'll tell it all."

And he did. He told it all from the moment when he had got off the airliner in Dublin, leaving out nothing except certain details of his relationship with Miss Rita Woolley which he considered were best kept to himself. And O'Higgins listened, listened with growing wonder and dismay and bewilderment.

When Fawley had completed his account the older man was silent for a whole minute, as if digesting the story and trying to come to terms with something so contrary to all his expectations.

Then he said: "I don't believe it. It can't be true; it just can not be true."

"Why would I lie to you?" Fawley said. "Why would I concoct such a tale? Where would be the point in it?"

Suddenly O'Higgins buried his face in his hands and his shoulders began to shake. If Fawley had not known it was impossible he would have said Uncle Danny was crying. He felt embarrassed; he wanted to get up and leave the room, leaving O'Higgins to his grief. But he did not move.

After a while O'Higgins seemed to take a hold on himself. He lowered his hands and stared at them, as though searching for something that should have been in them and was not.

He said slowly, not looking at Fawley: "There've been FBI agents here, you know."

"I didn't know," Fawley said. How could he have known? "What did they want?"

"They were asking questions. About guns and things. Some of the other boys have been questioned. They're worried."

Fawley remembered that hint of uneasiness he had noticed in the visitors. It seemed he had not imagined it.

"Will this mean trouble for you?"

"I don't know. They were very polite. But you never know with that sort, do you? They play their cards pretty close to the chest. They could be on to something."

Fawley could see that there had been a change in his uncle since he had been away. He seemed deflated, less ebullient, less sure of himself. And worried; oh, yes, undoubtedly worried.

"Well, Clyde," O'Higgins said, and this time he did look at Fawley, "it seems you're maybe wise to pull out. The way things are going it could be the best course to take. Have you any plans?"

Fawley shook his head. "I have to think. If it's okay with you I'd like to go up to the cabin and try to get things straight with myself. I need to be alone. We'll have another talk when I come back. What do you say?"

"Sure, sure." O'Higgins smiled wryly. "Nothing goes the way you mean it to, does it? All those fine plans we made; what's become of them?"

"Maybe they were the wrong plans."

"Maybe so. They seemed right at the time, though. But what the hell! Who can tell what's right and what's wrong? We're not gods, Clyde. We can make mistakes. When do you aim to leave?"

"Tomorrow morning."

"Well, take care of yourself, my boy; take good care of yourself."

"I'll try," Fawley said.

*

He drove to the cabin by the lake in the Adirondacks in the Mercedes sports car which O'Higgins had given him as a present on his last birthday. He was troubled by a niggling sense of guilt because Uncle Danny had given him so much, and now he had repaid this generosity with what must surely look to the old man as a kind of betrayal of trust. Yet it could hardly be argued that he, Clyde Fawley, was to blame; he had gone along with the plan as far as he could; but it had been a folly from the start. And then, the way things had turned out, he could not have gone on with it further even if he had wished. So why feel guilty about it? Nevertheless, he did.

The cabin by the lake was built in the traditional style, with log walls and a shingled roof; but there was more luxury inside than the early settlers of that wilderness would ever have dreamed about. It was reached by a road which weaved its undulating way between the pines and passed other cabins of various types, each one screened from the neighbours by sheltering belts of trees. This made it possible to imagine one was alone in the wild and far from other human habitation, although there was a general store within easy reach and even the possibility of running out of provisions was a threat that hardly needed to be taken seriously.

Fawley arrived in the afternoon and parked the Mercedes and moved in. It seemed odd being there without Uncle Danny; the man had always been so much a part of the place that one half expected to see him at any moment coming through a doorway or throwing a log on to the open fire. Fawley could not forget for a moment that this was just one more of O'Higgins's possessions which had been shared with him and of which he had had the benefit without ever giving anything in return except a promise, implied rather than spoken, to follow the way of life which the man had planned for him.

But all that was finished now. Now he had to break away; he could no longer go on taking without question the rich gifts that O'Higgins was only too happy to lavish on him. He could not do so for the simple reason that he no longer believed in anything that O'Higgins stood for. In the few

113

weeks he had been away from the United States he had learnt much about life, about himself. The method of teaching had been brutal but it had been effective, and things could never be the same again.

So he must make the break, get away, live his own life, accept no more hand-outs. It would mean, of course, that he would have to get a job, a real one and not the kind of sinecure he had held hitherto; but he was surely capable of doing that. If not he was worth nothing and deserved nothing.

On the third day he decided that he would quit the cabin the next morning and return to New York.

And that evening he had a visitor.

*

It was late and darkness had fallen. Fawley was sitting in an armchair and reading a book when he heard a car approaching. It came to a halt outside the cabin and he heard a door slam and footsteps on the front porch. Somebody hammered on the door and when he opened it he discovered a little man in a leather jacket and dark blue trousers standing outside.

"Good evening to you, Mr Fawley," the man said. "Maybe you'll not be remembering me?"

"I remember you very well, Mr Grady," Fawley said; and he was thinking that there were any number of people he would have been a good deal more delighted to find on his doorstep at that hour of the night. "What brings you up here?"

"I wanted to have a word with you," Grady said.

Fawley made no move to let him into the cabin. "I can't think of anything there'd be for you and me to talk about. Frankly, I don't think we have anything in common." He was wondering just how Grady had managed to find him, and he was not at all happy that he had. He had a feeling that a visit from this little thin-faced man boded no good at all for him.

"Well now," Grady said, "that's a matter of opinion. I'm sure if we put our minds to it we can find plenty of subjects we're both interested in. So why don't you open that door a little wider and let me in? It's not so warm as it might be out here."

That was true. There was a fresh breeze blowing off the lake and quite a nip in the air. Fawley could feel a shiver in his spine, but it had nothing to do with the breeze; it was the sight of Grady standing there and waiting to be invited in that put the chill into his blood.

"Why don't you tell me what it is you want to talk to me about? Then I can decide whether it's worth while letting you in."

"Now come on, Mr Fawley. Is that any way to treat an old friend of your uncle's who's come all this way just to see you? Is it reasonable, I ask you?"

Fawley had to admit that it was not reasonable. And he doubted whether Grady would go away even if he shut the door in his face. He would probably stay there and hammer on the woodwork until it became too much to bear. So why not listen to what he had to say and then tell him to go?

"Okay," he said grudgingly. "You'd better come in, I suppose. But don't make it a long stay because I want to get to bed."

"Oh, I promise you it won't take long," Grady said.

He stepped inside and Fawley closed the door.

Grady sat down without being invited to. He seemed to be very much at ease and he inspected the big room with obvious approval.

"Very nice. When it comes to roughing it in the wilds your uncle surely knows the way to take the hardship out of it. And that's the truth, so it is."

"Did he tell you I was here?" Fawley asked. It was really a superfluous question, since O'Higgins had been the only person who knew his whereabouts.

"Why sure he did," Grady said. "Who else?"

Fawley was surprised that Uncle Danny should have given the information. After all, he had particularly told him that he wished to be alone to think things over, and that surely implied that he wanted no visitors. But perhaps Grady had used his smooth Irish tongue to persuade O'Higgins to tell him what he wanted to know.

"So what's it all about?" Fawley asked.

But Grady seemed to be in no hurry to get to the point. He had made himself comfortable in the armchair and now he took out a cigarette and lighted it.

"You don't mind if I smoke?"

"It's a bit late to ask that, isn't it? You've already lit the damned thing."

"I could put it out if you object." Grady was being very polite. Perhaps a little too polite.

"No; go ahead. I don't suppose it'll kill me."

"That's true enough," Grady said; and he gave a laugh, as though the remark had tickled his sense of humour. "I suppose you often come up here? To get away from it all."

"Look," Fawley said, with a touch of impatience, "you didn't come knocking on my door at this time of night to inquire into my personal habits, did you?"

"No. You're quite right. Whether you come here often or not don't signify a thing. I've just arrived from London."

The abrupt announcement startled Fawley and he gave an involuntary jerk of the head.

"London!"

"That's right. London, England, as you say in this country. It seems to surprise you."

"What were you doing there?"

"It was business. There was a young woman I had to see. She had a complaint to make."

"I don't see what this has to do with me," Fawley said. But he did; he saw only too clearly; and it made him uneasy. He watched Grady warily, as one might watch a starving wolf one had inadvertently admitted to the house.

"Don't you, now?" Grady said. "Would that be the gospel truth you're telling me?"

"Why wouldn't it be?"

"Why! Because the young woman's name was Molly and the complaint was about you."

Fawley said nothing; he just stared at Grady.

"Ah!" Grady said. "I see you understand me now."

Still Fawley said nothing.

"She says you killed two friends of hers. One Patrick Duggan and the other Sean Connolly. Is that true?"

"No," Fawley said. "They were trying to kill me and they ran their car into a flooded pit."

"So you're saying it was accidental death?"

"Either that or suicide."

Grady pulled at his cigarette and his head was wreathed in smoke. "It won't do, you know. It won't do at all."

"I don't get you."

"Well, look at it this way; you're supposed to be dead and you're alive. And two good men of ours are dead because of you. Is that the way you repay our generosity in letting you into the organization?"

"Generosity! Is that what you call it?" Fawley was amazed at Grady's audacity. "Some generosity when your lot give orders to have me blown up with a bomb I'm supposed to deliver to Paddington Station."

Grady was cool. "Now there's another thing. You bungled that, I hear."

"Bungled it! Well, for Christ's sake! If anyone bungled it, it was those bastards, Duggan and Connolly. Or the people who gave the order. Because there was no need to get rid of me. I hadn't done anything."

"Are you saying you didn't inform about the arms shipment?"

"You know damn well I didn't."

"I know nothing of the sort," Grady said. "But I'll take your word for it."

Fawley looked at him suspiciously. It seemed far too prompt an acceptance of his denial. "You will?"

"Sure, I will. I can tell you're a truthful young feller. I'm a good judge of character."

"Well, then –"

Again Grady sucked at his cigarette, polluting the air of the room with his exhalation. "But it makes no difference, does it? There's still the matter of the two men you killed."

"Damn it! I didn't kill them."

"Molly says you did."

"She'd say anything. She tried to kill me. Did she tell you that?"

"Oh, yes. She says you slugged her. That's not much like a gentleman, hitting a woman."

"So I should have let her stick the knife in me, I suppose?"

"You have a point there," Grady admitted. He dropped the cigarette on the floor and stubbed it out with his heel. "You're a pretty resourceful man, aren't you, Mr Fawley? I make it three times you should've died and yet you managed to escape. Of course the first time it was plain luck, but the other times it was all your own work. And now there's a big question we have to ask ourselves, isn't there?"

Fawley kept his eye on Grady, not missing a move. "And what might that be?"

"Why, it's this. Can you do it a fourth time?"

Fawley saw the movement of Grady's right hand as it slipped in under the leather jacket, and he knew that this was the moment. He reacted swiftly, not waiting to see the gun that would surely be in Grady's hand when it reappeared. There was a marble figurine on the table beside the chair in which he was sitting; it had a sharp-edged rectangular base nearly one inch thick. He jumped up from the chair, grabbed the figurine and rushed at Grady.

Grady's right had was just reappearing when Fawley reached him, and in it was a stubby revolver. Fawley noticed this just as he brought the base of the figurine smashing down on Grady's head. There was a peculiar crunching sound as the skull cracked under the force of the blow, and almost in the same instant came the snap of the revolver. Grady must have pressed the trigger at the very moment when the lethal edge of the marble struck him.

To Fawley it seemed as if he had received a hammer blow in the left side. There was a searing pain in the region of the lower ribs, and he staggered back and collapsed on the floor. He knew what had happened; the bullet had entered his body in more or less the same place where Molly's knife had gouged him. But it had gone deeper and had inflicted a great deal more damage. How much damage he could not tell; but it was bad, he was sure of that. And the blood was pouring out and making a stain on the carpet.

He looked at Grady and saw that he had nothing more to fear from that quarter. Grady was hanging over an arm of the chair and his head was a mess. There was no need to feel his pulse to make sure he was dead; no one with a head in that condition could possibly be alive.

"Oh God!" Fawley muttered; he felt sick. "Oh my God!"

And then the whole room began to whirl like a merry-go-round and a moment later he had lost it.

Chapter Fourteen – IN THE CLEAR

When he came to he was still lying on the carpet and Grady was still hanging over the arm of the chair. Fawley was not sure how long he had been unconscious, but he guessed that it had not been many minutes. He was feeling terrible, but he knew that he had to do something for himself because there was nobody else around to do anything for him, and if he did nothing he was a goner; that was for sure.

He dragged himself to the chair in which he had been sitting, and with much effort and a deal of pain he managed to haul himself to his feet. He felt groggy, and he clung to the back of the chair and could feel the blood running down his thigh. Somehow he had to staunch that flow, and the first objective was to get to the bathroom. It took him some time, but he made it, clinging to anything on the way that would lend him support. In the bathroom he made a pad with a face towel and pushed it under his shirt and fixed it in place with a length of gauze bandage from the medical cabinet. Doing all this had taken a lot out of him; he felt weak and shaky and he had to sit down for a while to get a little strength back.

He knew that he had to get help; that was essential. And he had to leave the cabin because there was no telephone. O'Higgins had always maintained that there was no need for one; the cabin was a refuge from all the problems and distractions of life in New York and he wanted no one calling him up while he was on vacation. Which was all very well as long as nothing went wrong, but it made no allowance for emergencies.

There was an emergency right now and Fawley would have been damned glad of a telephone. He just wanted to lie down and wait for someone to come along and pick him up. He felt like death, but he had to make a move.

He got himself out of the bathroom and his eye was inevitably drawn to the gruesome sight of Michael Grady hanging over the arm of the chair. Fawley made it to his own chair and sat down for another rest. He looked at Grady and wondered why he had been chosen as the executioner. Perhaps because he had had dealings with O'Higgins and knew his way around.

Molly must have been pretty quick in getting in touch with her compatriots after her own failure, and they had wasted no time in sending Grady along to hear her story. He had probably gone to the hotel after that and discovered that his man had already departed, and it had been an easy guess that he had returned to the States. So Grady had bought himself an airline ticket and followed. And it might have been a whole lot better for him if he had not.

The blood was already soaking the towel when Fawley willed himself to get moving again. He reached the outer door and stood for a few seconds hanging on to the doorpost while the fresh breeze seemed to clear his head a little. Grady's car, a hired one, was standing outside, and Fawley's Mercedes was there as well. Somehow he had to get to it.

The trouble was that, having left the front porch, he had to walk a dozen yards or so with no support. He took a couple of wobbly steps and then his legs folded and he collapsed, giving his side a wrench that hurt like hell. He felt a strange desire to stay where he was, lying on the ground, but he could see that there was no future in that, and after a minute or two he began to crawl slowly towards the Mercedes on hands and knees.

He reached it at last and took the keys out of his pocket and opened the door and hauled himself on to the driver's seat. When he had got that far he again had the almost irresistible desire to do nothing more; his head was swimmy and he felt so damned weak. He wondered just how much blood he had lost and how much more he would be able to lose before he passed out. But the speculation was purposeless and he started the engine and set the car in motion.

He was seeing none too clearly and he had difficulty in keeping the car on the narrow twisting road. Trees kept coming at him and several times he was only inches away from a head-on crash. Blood was leaking through the towel and he felt a ridiculous concern for the upholstery, which he knew was just crazy. His brain was certainly not working as well as it should have been.

There were times when he doubted whether he would make it; the distance seemed to have increased tenfold over what it had always been before and the road appeared to go on for ever. But he got to the store at last, though he could only see it through a kind of mist that had drifted up between him and everything else, and he brought the Mercedes to a halt and just leaned on the horn and let it rip.

Somebody opened the door and looked in at him and said: "Jesus!"

Fawley was unable to see who it was because of the mist which was really thick now and getting thicker by the minute.

"Been shot," he mumbled. "Need a doctor. Bleeding –"

And then the mist became a fog and the fog was turning black and he just lost his hold and let it all go.

*

His father and mother came to visit him in hospital, and he was pleased to see them, though at first they seemed rather ill-at-ease and as if they hardly knew what to say.

Henry Fawley was as smooth and pale and soberly dressed as ever, but Clyde found that he no longer despised him for being as he was; he no longer compared him unfavourably with Uncle Danny; he saw that his father had many good qualities that O'Higgins did not possess.

Mrs Fawley pressed his hand and gazed at him with tears in her eyes. "We've been so worried about you, Clyde. When we heard you'd gone to Ireland we –"

Henry Fawley broke in: "Don't bother him with that now. How are you feeling, son?"

"I'll be okay," Clyde said. He wanted to ask about O'Higgins, but he hesitated to do so and neither his father nor his mother mentioned the man.

After a time they left and nothing of importance had been said. Clyde Fawley had a feeling that they were holding something back from him; that they knew something which he did not and were keeping it from him because of his condition. And it was so unnecessary, since although the bullet from Michael Grady's revolver had chipped a rib and made quite a mess of him, his condition was far from critical and he was quite fit enough to take any kind of revelation without risk of injury to his health.

A police detective visited his bedside and questioned him about the incident at the cabin. Fawley kept a guard on his tongue and professed ignorance of the reason why Grady had tried to kill him. He told the officer that Grady was an acquaintance of his uncle's and he had first met the man in O'Higgins's house. The detective asked if he knew what kind of business Grady was engaged in. Fawley said he did not.

He was bothered by the fact that he had no idea what O'Higgins had told the police; for they would surely have interviewed him. But he had to play it the best way he could, and a profession of ignorance seemed to be the most favourable ploy.

With regard to the killing of Michael Grady he appeared to be in the clear. It was a pretty obvious case of self-defence, since Grady's fingerprints were on the revolver and it had been fired and the slug had undoubtedly entered Fawley's body.

He was puzzled by the fact that O'Higgins had not been to see him. Though he had disappointed his uncle he would not have imagined that to be a sufficient reason for the man to stay away from him. But perhaps he had a feeling of guilt for having directed Grady to the lakeside cabin and could not face his nephew.

When his parents paid a second visit to Fawley he put the question directly to them.

"Is Uncle Danny okay?"

Henry Fawley seemed disconcerted by the inquiry. "Why do you ask?"

"I thought he'd have been to see me, but he hasn't. Is he ill?"

Mrs Fawley gave her husband a meaning glance. "Don't you think you'd better tell him? He has to know sometime."

"What do I have to know?" Clyde asked. "Tell me."

Henry Fawley gave a faint sigh. "I'm afraid your uncle is dead."

"Dead!" Clyde could hardly believe it. "But how? I mean –"

Henry Fawley cleared his throat nervously. "It seems he shot himself."

Clyde stared at him. "What do you mean – seems. You must know whether he did or not."

"Well, yes, he did."

"But why would he do a thing like that? What reason did he have?"

"It was probably to avoid going to jail."

"Jail! Surely there wasn't any danger of that."

"Apparently there was. Proceedings were about to be brought against him on a charge of illegal arms trafficking. Some of his buddies have been arrested; McNulty, Mitchell and a few others. They've been active, it seems, in supplying guns and explosives to the Provisional IRA." Henry Fawley gave his son an inquiring glance. "I don't suppose you knew anything about that?"

Clyde shook his head. There was no point in telling his parents just how much he had known, how much he had been involved; it would only have pained them. And luckily there was nothing he had done that the FBI could get him for.

122

"I'm glad," Fawley said. "I guess your uncle couldn't face the possibility of being arrested, and so he took the only way out. An unsavoury business. Most distasteful."

When Mr and Mrs Fawley had gone Clyde thought about that unsavoury and distasteful business. He had no doubt that his father had been correct regarding the reason for Uncle Danny's suicide. He remembered what O'Higgins had said that last time he had seen him; that he had had a visit from Federal Agents. He had been a worried man and had probably felt hunted. Yes, that was almost certainly why he had taken his own life.

Yet could there perhaps have been another reason? He had undoubtedly directed Michael Grady to the place where he, Clyde Fawley, had been staying. And he must have known what Grady's purpose was even if the Irishman had not spelled it out for him. After what Clyde had told him about the attempts on his life in England O'Higgins could have had no difficulty in guessing why Grady wished to find his nephew.

Clyde could picture the scene in the big house on Riverside Drive. Grady would have hauled out the revolver and threatened to shoot O'Higgins if he refused to give the information. And Uncle Danny must have caved in and given it; because maybe in spite of all the bluster and the bravado he had been nothing better than a chicken-heart and a bladder of wind when it came to the crunch.

So was the true reason for the suicide there? Men had killed themselves in fits of remorse before this. And might not Daniel Reilly O'Higgins have added one more to the number?

Perhaps. But he would never know.

Chapter Fifteen – NOT INSUPERABLE

Fawley had some difficulty in finding Rita Woolley when he returned to London. He tried the hospital where he had visited her and was given an address. It turned out to be a dreary lodging-house where a blowsy woman wearing a spotted pinafore and smoking a cigarette answered his inquiry.

"Rita Woolley. Oh, yes, I remember. She was here but she left. No, love, I don't know where she went. I meanter say, them young people they move around, don't they? 'Ere today and gone tomorrer, as the saying is."

He tried Raven House but found it still unoccupied; it looked as if the repair work had not even started. Perhaps in the end the old house would simply be demolished and something else would be built on the site.

He could have gone to the police and made inquiries about Miss Woolley; maybe they would have some information regarding her whereabouts. But he was reluctant to get involved with them again and he held back. Eventually he might apply to the constabulary as a last resort; but not yet.

It was a strange compulsion that drew him to the builder's yard. He knew that it might be unwise to be seen in that vicinity, but he went nevertheless. He wondered whether Molly was still living in the house, but when he got there he saw that the old sign had been taken down and a new one put up which read: B. B. Builders.

It occurred to him that this might be another front for an IRA cell; perhaps Molly had joined up with some other men and the activities were going on much as before. But he decided not to inquire; it would be foolish to press his luck too far.

It was a kind of nostalgia that drew him to the discotheque where he had gone with Rita that evening when she had persuaded him to accompany her in the pursuit of pleasure and a little joy. He had no expectation of finding her there; that would have been too much to hope for. But he thought he might capture some fleeting memory of that earlier visit, which had been in its way a kind of turning-point in his life.

When he walked in it seemed that nothing had changed; the lights, the glitter, the ear-splitting sound of the music, even the dancers, all seemed

124

the same. The difference was that there was no Miss Woolley dancing with him, smiling at him, shouting in his ear to make herself heard above the din. After a moment he knew that it had been a mistake to come: though he had expected nothing it was a disappointment nevertheless. In all the crush and the babel the place seemed empty without her.

He turned to go and felt a touch on his arm. He glanced at the hand, at the arm, at the shoulder, at the girl.

"Clyde!" she said. "Is it really you?"

"It's me," Fawley said. He could see the delight in her eyes and he felt his own heart leap at the sight of her. "Oh, sure it's me."

They were jostled by the crowd, pressed close against each other, face to face.

"Are you with anyone?" he asked, hating to think that she might be.

"No," she said. "I was waiting for you."

She had to be joking, of course. She could not have known that he would be there. But perhaps she had come for the same reason he had, to recapture something from the past. And luck had been with them both.

"And I was looking for you."

"You were?" Again the delight, the happiness in her eyes and in her voice. "You mean it?"

"I mean it."

She had the scar on her forehead. Some people might have said it marred her looks, but he would not have been one of them. She knew he was looking at it.

"It makes me a witch, doesn't it?"

"No," he said. "Nothing could make you a witch. Not for me."

They were jostled again.

"Let's get out of here," he said. "Let's go where we can talk without shouting."

They went to the coffee bar; it was another place that carried memories for them.

"So you came back," she said. "You came back after all."

"I said I would, didn't I?"

"Yes, but I didn't believe it. I hoped you would but it seemed so unlikely. I cried."

"You cried for me?"

"Yes, for you."

"I love you for that," he said. "But in future you must always believe what I say."

"Is there going to be a future?"

"You bet," Fawley said. "You bet your sweet life there is."

They drank some coffee and looked at each other, remembering.

"How would you like to marry an American millionaire?" Fawley asked.

She laughed. "I'd like it fine. But where would I find one?"

"You're looking at one right now."

She stared at him uncertainly. "You're kidding, aren't you. You are just kidding?"

"No kidding," Fawley said. "My Uncle Danny just died and left me all he had."

"And he had a million?"

"Give or take a few thousand."

"My!" she said; and her eyes widened. "Are you going to propose to me?"

"I thought I just did."

She leaned over and kissed him. "Do you really want me to marry you?"

"Of course I do. Why else would I have come back?"

"Oh dear!" she said. "If I accept you now you'll never be sure whether I'm doing it for love or for money."

"That's true," Fawley said. "But I don't think it's an insuperable obstacle to wedlock, do you?"

She thought about it for a few seconds with a little pucker in her forehead. Then suddenly she smiled and kissed him again.

"No, Clyde darling, it's not insuperable."

"I'm glad," Fawley said. "Because without you I just wouldn't know what to do with the money."